HEARTSIDE BAY

More
Than a
Love
Song

CATHY COLE

■SCHOLASTIC

Scholastic Children's Books
An imprint of Scholastic Ltd
Euston House, 24 Eversholt Street, London, NW1 1DB, UK
Registered office: Westfield Road, Southam, Warwickshire, CV47 0RA
SCHOLASTIC and associated logos are trademarks and/or registered
trademarks of Scholastic Inc.

First published in the UK by Scholastic Ltd, 2014

Text copyright © Scholastic Ltd, 2014

ISBN 978 1407 14048 3

A CIP catalogue record for this book is available
from the British Library.

Printed by CPI Group (UK) Ltd, Croydon, CR0 4YY
Papers used by Scholastic Children's Books are made
from wood grown in sustainable forests.

1 3 5 7 9 10 8 6 4 2

This is a work of fiction. Names, characters, places,
incidents and dialogues are products of the author's imagination
or are use fictitiously. Any resemblance to actual people, living
or dead, events or locales is entirely coincidental.

www.scholastic.co.uk

HEARTSIDE BAY

THE **HEARTSIDE BAY** SERIES

With love to Lucy Courtenay and Sara Grant

ONE

Gazing out over the audience of the undead, Rhi felt like she was going to throw up. Her hands were shaking, and her heart was racing. What was she doing here?

This is all a terrible mistake.

Below her on the dance floor, people were chattering and laughing. They were an unusual crowd in bloodied suits, tattered dresses and gruesomely painted faces. Whose idea had it been to have a zombie-themed wedding? It wasn't what Rhi would have called romantic.

Her heart gave a tug. It was probably just as well, she thought miserably. Right now, romance was the last thing she needed reminding of.

"Give us a song then!" a green-skinned corpse

shouted out from the back of the room, interrupting Rhi's chaotic train of thought.

The chatter died down. The bride and groom – the most ghoulish pair in the room – took their positions for the first dance. And every eyeball in the room, bloodshot and otherwise, turned to face Rhi.

If possible, Rhi's throat got even drier. Swallowing didn't help. Wringing her hands, she directed an agonized glare in the direction of her two best friends, Lila and Polly, who were grinning and giving her the thumbs-up from the safety of the catering area. How had this happened? How had she allowed them to talk her up here, on to the stage? She was supposed to be waitressing.

Mr Gupta's catering company specialized in themed weddings, ranging from *Hello Kitty* to *Star Trek*. "You need to start showing a bit more responsibility," Rhi's mum had said. "Heartside Bay has a *lot* of weddings. And you need to start saving for university if you're going to do anything with your life, Rhi! Waitressing for Mr Gupta will only take up a few days a month, and it won't interfere with your schoolwork." Schoolwork was a big thing for Rhi's mum. In the end,

Rhi had talked Lila and Polly into joining her, and here they were at their first event. Half an hour earlier, Rhi had been setting out ghoulish wedding canapés – quails' eggs painted to look like eyeballs, skinny witch's-finger sausages with carrot-flake fingernails, red apple sliced and neatly arranged above and below fang-like marshmallow teeth – when Lila had grabbed her arm. Rhi had almost dropped the tray.

Lila's blue eyes were blazing with excitement through the red eyeliner that all the waitresses were wearing to make them fit with the theme. Rhi didn't like the look on her friend's face.

"What?" she said cautiously.

Lila had given a pointed nod in the direction of the wedding manager.

Mr Gupta was pacing up and down the grey, tattered-looking marquee with his phone clamped to his ear. "What do you *mean* the wedding singer can't make it?" he was hissing into the receiver. He mopped his sweating forehead with a large, damp-looking handkerchief. "They're supposed to be on in *twenty minutes*! You're killing me here!"

Rhi had a strange, creeping feeling. She opened

her mouth and licked her lips, which had grown unaccountably dry. "What has a missing wedding singer got to do with me?" she said feebly.

Lila rolled her eyes as if Rhi had said something incredibly stupid. "Do I have to spell it out for you? You've wanted to be a singer for practically your whole life."

"No," said Rhi in panic.

Lila looked at her disbelievingly. "You *don't* want to be a singer? That's the first I've heard of it. I've known you for a long time, remember?"

"No, I do . . . I don't. . ."

Lila cut through Rhi's frantic stuttering. "This is your moment. Get up there and sing. Help Mr Gupta and show the world what you can do!"

Rhi was so shocked, she could barely speak. "Lila, I sing in my bedroom in front of my mirror," she managed. "But that is *not* the same thing as singing for a room full of hundreds of zombies. I'm not ready to sing in front of all these people. I'm here to waitress and that's . . . Lila? *Lila!*"

Lila was already walking towards Mr Gupta.

"Mr Gupta!" she called. "Rhi can sing for you."

Mr Gupta shoved his phone into his pocket. "What? Rhi who?" He clocked Rhi standing frozen over her tray of canapés. "Is she any good?"

"She sings like an angel," Lila assured him. "She plays the guitar too."

"To be honest, I don't care if she croaks like a frog," Mr Gupta said, wiping his forehead again. "We need a singer. Will you do it, Rhi?"

Polly appeared through the catering area curtain. She was wearing a tattered gothic dress and blood-stained apron with a slash of bright red lipstick and bloodied eye make-up, and somehow looked ten times cooler than every guest in the room.

"Is Rhi going to sing?" she said in excitement, setting down her tray and wiping her hands on her apron. "Mr Gupta, she's amazing. The guests are going to love her."

"I can't!" Rhi squeaked in horror.

"Of course you can," said Lila, Polly and Mr Gupta all at the same time.

"I will pay you extra," said Mr Gupta desperately. He checked his watch and muttered under his breath, then pulled a list of songs from his pocket and thrust them at Rhi. "The playlist. The band will know what to do."

Rhi stared at the band, who were already tuning up.

"What's the worst that can happen?" Lila said in a coaxing voice, pulling off Rhi's apron. "You already look amazing in that outfit."

"One of my better efforts, I have to say," Polly added, smoothing down the old silver-grey satin dress that she'd adapted for Rhi with a ripped hemline.

"Plus," Lila added helpfully, "the audience is already dead."

Polly had laughed, fluffed up Rhi's cloudy dark hair one more time and pushed her towards the stage. And now here she was. Facing her doom.

She felt someone tap her on the arm.

"What are we starting with then?" asked the keyboard player, sounding bored.

Rhi held the playlist towards him with nerveless fingers. "The first one, I guess."

The opening chords of "Endless Love" rippled from the keyboard. The audience fell still.

This is it, Rhi thought hopelessly. *There is no*

escape. And of all the songs, it had to be "Endless Love".

There had been nothing endless about her and Max. He had killed their relationship by going off with Rhi's friend Eve behind Rhi's back. With her heart hurting, she closed her eyes and started to sing.

As she sang, she lost herself in the music, and in the images that the words conjured. Her first kiss with Max on the clifftops, the wind buffeting them as they held tightly to each other and laughed and kissed and laughed again. . . The way he had looked at her as if she were the only girl in the room. . .

How had it gone so wrong? She and Max had been so perfect, until Eve had stolen him away. Eve would get bored of him soon, surely? Then Rhi would win him back. She and Max were *meant* to be together. What was left of them, at least. They were as tattered as the wedding dress the zombie bride was wearing.

With tears blurring her eyes, Rhi put her heart and soul into the music.

She did everything she could do to keep it together until the last note.

As the music died away and she bowed her head, Rhi was dimly aware of the silence.

Great, she thought, not daring to open her eyes. *My first public performance and I blow it.*

TWO

The room erupted.

Rhi opened her eyes and stared at the crowd in bewilderment. People were calling, whistling and cheering. Stamping their feet and punching their hands in the air. Cries of "More!" and "Give us another one!" echoed around the marquee. She had to resist the urge to turn around and check for someone else, a real singer, who had got the crowd as pumped as this. It was unbelievable that all this was for her.

There was a whistle behind her. Rhi spun round.

"Nice," said the keyboard player, giving her a wink.

"Whoo!" Polly screamed. "Go Rhi!"

"Told you you could do it!" Lila shouted.

Still the crowd was cheering and calling for more

songs. Rhi put her hands to her burning cheeks and drank in this glorious moment. Lila was right. All her life, she had dreamed of writing and singing songs. It had seemed impossible. But now . . . this. . .

The keyboard player kicked off with the next track and she was singing again. The whole zombie-filled room swayed and sang with her.

I don't need Max, she thought. *I just need this.*

"You were incredible," Lila enthused when, at last, Rhi left the stage to wild applause.

"You have to do it professionally, Rhi," Polly added earnestly. "Do you have any idea how good you were up there?"

All Rhi knew was that she had loved every second. Her head was whirling.

"I have put an extra fifty pounds in your wage packet, Rhi," said Mr Gupta warmly. "Let me know if you ever want to sing at my weddings again. I am sure I can arrange it."

Rhi needed peace and quiet to take all this in. "Thank you, Mr Gupta," she managed. She turned to her friends. "Was it really OK?"

"It was more than OK," said Polly. "It was spine-tingling."

"I told you it was a good idea," crowed Lila.

Breathe, Rhi instructed herself. It was surprisingly hard to do. The room was too loud, and the crowd was still craning their necks, looking at her and talking about her.

"I have to go to the bathroom," she blurted, and hurried away before the others could stop her.

In the quiet of the toilets, she rested her head against the mirror and relived that amazing moment when the room had cheered for her singing. She brushed her thick black hair away from her face and studied her reflection in wonder.

She hardly recognized the person staring back at her. The pearly grey satin seemed to give her dark skin an extra glow, and her warm almond-brown eyes looked bright and radiant. It was like she had been plugged into something that had lit her up like a Christmas tree.

She had just sung in front of a crowd of people and they had loved it. She wanted to do it again, and again, and again. If only she could make this her life.

But you can't, she reminded herself. *This was fun, but that's all it is. Like Mum says, life is serious.*

She was surprised at the grief she felt.

Lila put her head round the toilet door. "Everything OK? People are asking for the singing waitress out there. Mr Gupta sent me to get you."

Rhi smoothed her hair one more time. It sprang back into its usual cloud around her face. "Sorry. I'll be out in a minute."

The disco had kicked in now. Rhi moved around the marquee with Lila and Rhi, offering blood-coloured champagne to the guests and smiling shyly every time someone complimented her on her singing.

It was a long evening. After the champagne, there was food to hand round, plates to clear and glasses to fill. Still floating, Rhi kept her head down and worked harder than she'd ever worked in her life.

Close to midnight, the last guests started heading out through the artfully tattered marquee door, covering yawns with the backs of their hands. On Mr Gupta's instructions, Polly started sweeping the dance floor and Lila and Rhi cleared the remaining tables. As she stacked plates and listened to Lila's chatter, Rhi let herself drift back in time to the start of the evening when she was still up on the stage. The memory was intoxicating.

"What's with the waitressing?"

One of the remaining guests was leaning over a table towards Rhi. He was wearing a battered top hat, a pair of bloody gloves hung in shredded tatters from his hands, and his face was painted to look like a skull.

"You were the wedding singer, right?" he said.

"It was a last-minute thing," Rhi said shyly. "I usually just waitress."

"She was incredible, wasn't she?" Lila chimed in, putting her arm round Rhi's shoulders. "She plays the guitar as well!"

"Lila," Rhi protested, reddening. If she was nervous about her singing, it was nothing compared to how she felt about playing guitar. She'd inherited the instrument from her sister, so playing it was especially personal.

The top-hatted guy didn't seem interested in her guitar-playing. "What's your name?" he asked.

Rhi giggled. She couldn't help it. How were you

supposed to talk seriously to a guy who looked like a zombie? "Rhi."

He patted his grubby, bloodstained waistcoat and pulled a card from a pocket. "Well, Rhi, I'm Dave Dubois. I'm a talent scout. You should give me a call."

Rhi stared at the card he was holding out.

"Rhi would love that," Lila said, taking the card from his hand. "Wouldn't you, Rhi?"

Rhi shook her head, trying to clear her mind. "Er, yes. Thanks. Really?"

She took the card from Lila and studied it. The black card was a bit bent, like it had been sitting in the guy's pocket for a while.

Dave Dubois made a sort of gun shape with his fingers. "Call me. We could do business."

Rhi didn't know what to say. She hadn't been expecting this. "Don't joke," she said awkwardly.

"It's no joke. Don't lose that card now. I'm your ticket to fame and glory, babe."

He flicked the grubby brim of his top hat in farewell and headed out through the tent flap into the night.

"Oh my GOD!" Lila squealed when he'd gone.

14

She snatched the card back from Rhi and looked at it properly. "You've just been spotted, Rhi!"

Rhi felt dizzy. This kind of thing didn't happen, especially not to someone like her. People from Heartside Bay didn't end up being talent spotted for music careers. It was all what her mother would call a silly dream.

Wasn't it?

THREE

Rhi tried not to yawn. Last night had been exciting, but exhausting too, and the last thing she felt like doing was being here at the Heartbeat Café with everyone.

It wasn't because the Heartbeat was a bad place to hang out. It was the best spot in Heartside, with a big stage and live music slots and walls carved with love messages and initials from couples down the years. The music was great and everyone came here after school and at weekends. But all she wanted right now was to be in her cosiest PJs, curled up in bed with her guitar and remembering the magic of the previous night.

The whole Heartside gang was out tonight,

and Lila had demanded Rhi come along. Rhi hadn't been happy when she walked in and saw not only Polly, Lila and her boyfriend Ollie, but also Eve and Max. Lila had given Rhi a guilty look but it was too late to leave now. It had only been a week since everyone had made up over the whole two-timing business, and Rhi still found it hard to be in the same room with her former best friend and boyfriend. She wondered if it would ever get easier.

She reminded herself that this was better than when everyone was fighting. During that time the tension, especially between Eve and Lila, had been unbearable. She would have to cope with the situation as best she could. She wouldn't let Max know how much she still missed him, even after everything he had done to her. She had her pride.

Eve kissed Max and whispered something in his ear that made him laugh. Rhi turned her head away and tried to catch Polly's eye. She could really use a conversation to take her mind off what was happening opposite.

Polly was staring at her lap, smoothing out her

skirt in the strange concentrated way she had when she was stressed. On Rhi's other side, Lila and Ollie were teasing each other, but the teasing had a barbed undertone to it.

"Thanks to that extra football practice you never told me about, I felt like a total loser waiting on the beach for you this morning. . ."

"I knew you'd be mad and I didn't want to upset you. . ."

"Standing me up on the beach wasn't upsetting?"

"The gulls kept you company, right? I sent them along especially."

"You're impossible. . ."

Rhi felt uneasy. She had always thought Lila and Ollie were the perfect couple. They were both so good-looking and constantly cheerful. Maybe she was wrong. She wondered why good things always had to change.

She turned her eyes to the scarred wooden wall beside their booth. It was plastered in love messages carved by visitors to the Heartbeat Café. Lifting her fingers, she traced a little heart with the date "1961" carefully inscribed in the centre. It was wonderful, thinking about all the happiness that this little café had seen over the years.

Her eyes drifted further up the panelling. Scratched into a small space just beneath the wall lamp that lit their booth, she read the message *MH & RW 4ever*. Her heart twisted. Max Holmes had a funny sense of for ever. They had been so happy just a few weeks ago. It was all Eve's fault that she and Max had gone wrong. Eve had dazzled him with her confidence and money, and he'd forgotten what he and Rhi had had together. How could she get Eve to leave Max alone? She wanted him back so desperately, she was afraid the whole café could read it in her eyes.

Someone was tapping the mic to get the room's attention.

Ryan Jameson's long brown hair flopped into his eyes as usual as he leaned in to the microphone on the stage. For as long as Rhi been coming to the Heartbeat Café, Ryan's hair had been too long. Rhi guessed his parents were probably too busy running this place to remind him to get his hair cut.

"Right, so hi, everyone," Ryan began. "Welcome

to Open Mic Night."

There were a few whoops at this.

"I want to introduce an exciting new talent to the stage tonight. Please give a warm Heartbeat welcome to . . . Brody Baxter!"

A tall blond guy came on to the stage holding a battered guitar. The guitar appeared to be covered in fruit stickers – the kind Rhi recognized from bananas and apples. It looked pretty cool. Rhi wondered if she could do something like that with Ruth's guitar, then decided she couldn't. In her heart, she still felt like she had her sister's guitar on loan.

"Um, hey," said Brody down the microphone. "How are you all?"

There was a loud cheer. Rhi noticed that girls all round the room had stopped what they were doing and were focusing all their attention on the stage. There was no doubt about it: Brody was hot. From their table near the stage, Rhi could see that his eyes were clear crystal blue, fringed with thick dark lashes. He tossed his long, sun-bleached locks out of his eyes and leaned over the neck of his guitar, tweaking the tuning pegs until the strings sang pure and mellow beneath his fingers.

"He's cute," said Lila.

"Hey," Ollie objected.

"And I bet he doesn't stand girls up on beaches," Lila added.

Ollie looked sour. "How do you know?"

Brody leaned into the mic again. His voice was deep and a little hoarse.

"I'd like to sing something I wrote a while back. It's called 'Be With Me'."

Rhi sat up, intrigued. She'd assumed this guy would sing cover songs like most of the acts who performed at the Heartbeat. You had to be a brave person to sing your own stuff in front of this crowd. Rhi thought about her own songbook, scrawled and scribbled until the pages had worn thin, tucked safely under her mattress. It was full of all the deeply private, personal things she had felt since Ruth died, and found herself only able to express in songs. She couldn't imagine ever being brave enough to sing them in public.

"Be with me," Brody sang. He closed his eyes so his lashes lay like dark feathers on his cheeks. "I know you're hurt, dragged in the dirt, let me lift you in my arms and carry you from here, from all the hate and all the fear, be with me, be with me. . ."

Rhi felt like she was being transported into Brody's soul.

"I feel your pain, I feel it too, kiss me again, know I'm with you, we'll see it through. . . Be with me, be with me."

He sang the words softly but certainly, holding the silent room in the palm of his hand. Tears pricked Rhi's eyelids as he changed key with deft fingers, taking the song to an even deeper and more emotional plane.

"Be with me, lie with me, die with me, for ever. . . Be with me, lie with me, die with me, for ever. . ."

The closing chorus was taken up by half the crowd, who began to sing along. Rhi couldn't have joined in if she had wanted to. Her throat was too choked.

"Be . . . with me," Brody Baxter finished.

A perfect moment of silence hung over the room before the room rocked with applause. Rhi clapped until her hands hurt.

Brody played one called "Fast Lane Freak" next. It

wasn't about girls or parties or money. Instead it was the story of a guy living by the side of the road, eking out an existence from the things people threw from their car windows. "Trash and cash is all the same, everyone ride that gravy train, breathe the fumes and breathe the fame, I'm a fast lane freak, I ain't ashamed, I ain't ashamed. . ."

Rhi found herself laughing along with the rest of the room at the sly pokes about life in the modern world that Brody Baxter had put in his song. He was exactly the kind of singer/songwriter she wanted to be.

After two more songs, he gave a little bow. "More laters," he said into the mic.

Applause crashed like thunder around the room.

"Wow," Rhi said breathlessly as he headed off stage with a brief wave. She felt like she had been breathing stardust. "Don't you think he was awesome?"

"He was OK," said Max with a shrug.

Rhi felt a flash of annoyance on Brody's behalf. Max said the dumbest things sometimes. How could she still feel so much for him?

"You should duet with him, Rhi," said Lila suddenly. "I'm sure Ryan could fix you two up. Rhi sang this amazing set at a wedding we waitressed for last night," she told the others before Rhi could stop her. "You should have heard her!"

Rhi could feel herself flushing. "It was just a one-off thing."

Eve arched her eyebrows. "Since when do waitresses sing at weddings?" She couldn't have sounded more patronizing if she tried.

"Since this weekend," said Polly defiantly. "She even had a talent scout come up to her at the end and give her his card!"

Rhi had tucked Dave Dubois's card into her jeans for good luck that morning. She'd taken it out several times today to look at it, in case it had magically turned blank in the night. She still didn't know if she had the guts to ring him.

Eve rolled her eyes. "You are so naive. He was probably a sleaze with no connections at all. Or he gave Rhi his card just to be nice. No one gets spotted at *weddings*."

Rhi was feeling more embarrassed by the moment.

"I'm going to get a drink," she mumbled, standing up from the table and heading for the bar. She could feel her cheeks burning with humiliation. Eve was such a cow.

Ryan was behind the bar, fiddling with the espresso machine. Although he was in most of her classes, Rhi didn't know him all that well. He tended to hang around the edges of their group, looking for a way in to their conversations. She wasn't even sure who his real friends were.

"Hey," he said, glancing up at her through his overlong fringe. "What can I get you?"

"A frappé please," said Rhi. She glanced back at the table. Her friends were clearly still arguing about her. She caught Max's eye and looked away quickly.

"Does Lila want anything?" Ryan asked. He rubbed his ear. "You know, like my heart on a plate?"

Ryan had clearly had a crush on Lila for weeks. Rhi had seen the way he looked over at their table in lunch break and hung around the lockers at the end of the day on the off-chance he'd bump into her.

"I don't think so," she said, smiling as kindly as she could.

"Love sucks," Ryan sighed.

Rhi glanced back at Max. His arm was round Eve and he was whispering something in her ear. "Tell me about it," she said drily.

The smell of freshly brewed espresso filled the air. "Unrequited for you too, huh?" Ryan asked with interest.

It's more complicated than that, thought Rhi unhappily.

Watching Ryan blitz the ice for her frappé, she suddenly had an idea. If Max saw her buddying up to Ryan, he might get jealous and realize what he was missing. She wasn't proud of the thought, but couldn't ignore the opportunity.

She lowered her voice and leaned over the bar. "Do me a favour, will you?"

Ryan pushed her frappé towards her. "Name it."

Rhi squirmed a little. She had to do it. Now.

"Act like I just said something really funny," she said in slight desperation.

Ryan looked surprised. "Uh, why?"

Rhi risked a glance under her arm. Max was looking in their direction with a faint frown on his face. It was now or never.

"Just do it, would you?" she pleaded.

Ryan laughed loudly. Rhi tossed her hair, feeling a bit clumsy. She didn't dare look back at Max again.

"You're really pretty, you know," said Ryan. He reached out a hand and tugged on one of Rhi's dark curls. "You should make imaginary jokes more often."

Rhi peeked back at their table. Max looked jealous, there was no doubt about it. He always got a little crease between his eyebrows when he was annoyed about something.

"Hey," said Eve, tweaking Max's nose for his attention.

Max broke eye contact with Rhi and smiled into Eve's eyes. Eve's eyes flickered towards Rhi as she planted a loud kiss on Max's lips, making him laugh and pull her closer to him.

It looked as if Eve had won this particular battle.

With a sigh, Rhi pushed some change over the counter towards Ryan, picked up her frappé and headed back to the table. As she approached, Eve wriggled out from beneath Max's arm and hopped on to the stage.

"Hey everyone," she said sweetly down the microphone. "We have a real treat for you tonight. My best friend, Rhiannon Wills, is going to sing a duet with Brody Baxter. Everyone give it up!"

FOUR

Rhi stood paralysed as the whole room started clapping and cheering and standing on tiptoes to get a look at her. Brody had been pushed on to the stage with his guitar, and was shading his eyes to hunt out his surprise duet partner down on the café floor.

It was like the zombie wedding all over again, only worse. That had been singing to a room full of strangers. This would be singing to a room full of *friends*. It was too terrifying to think about.

"Don't be shy now." Tucking her long red hair back behind her ears, Eve leaned a little closer to the microphone. "She's over there, folks. Let's give her a hand up here."

Rhi wanted to die as Eve smirked at her from the stage.

You've made your point, she wanted to shout as hands reached for her, pushing her towards the steps. *I get it. Max is yours. Don't make me do this. . .*

But then she was up the steps, blinking in the bright lights, and Eve was back at the table among Rhi's cheering friends, and Brody was smiling quizzically at her.

"You sing?" he said.

What was she supposed to say? Yes, in my bedroom? Once in a room full of zombies?

"I guess," she whispered.

Brody strummed his fingers lightly across the guitar strings as the audience shouted "Duet!" at them both.

"I'm really sorry," Rhi mumbled. This was the most humiliating thing that had ever happened to her. "It wasn't my idea to crash your set. Eve can be . . . kind of forceful."

"Don't worry about it," Brody replied. He considered her with an appreciative smile. "I'd love to sing a duet with the most beautiful girl in Heartside."

Rhi felt as if she was blushing all over. He was even

better-looking up close. His skin was tanned, and his eyes were like perfect sunlit pools of warm blue water. She couldn't quite believe she was standing next to him on the stage. She felt as shy as if he were some rock star she'd had a crush on for years.

"So what's it going to be?" Brody asked, raising his eyebrows.

Rhi swallowed. "Um, do you know 'The One That Got Away'?"

Brody's eyes flashed with interest. "Ready when you are."

He plucked the opening notes on his guitar. Rhi looked at Max and Eve, sitting with their heads close together. *Max got away, that's for sure,* she thought numbly.

She began to sing.

Brody kept pace with her on his guitar, plucking the strings as Rhi's voice built towards the chorus. Then he lifted his head and joined in with the harmony.

Rhi felt a shock of wonder. The combination of sound was electric. As if somehow her voice had broken into two parts, pure and high at the top and soft and husky at the bottom. Emotion matched emotion, each note was perfectly balanced against the other.

There was a natural give and take as they sang. Somehow Rhi knew what Brody was going to do before he did it. She'd never experienced anything like it. The Heartbeat Café faded to nothing. It was just her, Brody and the song.

As she reached the last note, Rhi opened her eyes in a kind of daze. She had been drawing closer and closer to Brody over the one microphone they had been sharing until their faces were millimetres apart. She could feel the heat of him. She could almost touch his cheek with her lips.

Rhi turned her head towards Brody at the same moment he turned his towards hers. They stared at each other for a single long electric second. And all Rhi could think was:

I want to kiss him.

She jerked her head back, breaking the spell. She had let herself get carried away by the song. She hadn't really been thinking of kissing Brody, had she? She could feel his eyes still on her.

A roar of applause swept across the room, breaking

through her confused emotions. Lila had put two fingers in her mouth and was whistling. Ollie and Polly were both clapping hard, their hands held high above their heads. Eve looked put out that her stunt had backfired on her so spectacularly. And Max. . .

Her ex-boyfriend was staring at her with wide eyes like he'd never seen her before.

Rhi turned back to Brody. "Thanks," she said wonderingly. "I enjoyed that."

He smiled into her eyes. Rhi found herself wanting to dive into their clear blue depths. "I should thank you," he said. "You can sing with me any time." And he kissed her cheek.

The crowd was still applauding, drumming the floor with their feet and the tables with their hands. Laughing, Rhi raised her hands in appreciation. Her face felt like it would split in half from smiling too much. She hadn't felt this alive in years.

She always felt that a part of her had died with Ruth after the car accident. Now for the first time she could feel that part of her blossoming back to life. Maybe it was time to put the past behind her. Maybe it was time to live again. To live properly this time.

Not the way her parents wanted her to. The way *she* wanted.

Dave Dubois's card crinkled in her pocket. With a rush of sudden resolve, Rhi decided to phone him. *I'll do it tonight,* she thought. *When I've worked up enough nerve I'll call him and arrange to meet him.* Could she really have a singing career? Based on the crowd's reaction tonight, and the wedding's reaction the previous day, maybe . . . just maybe she could. She had never dared let herself think that it was possible.

But now, for the first time, she saw a glimmer of hope.

FIVE

Rhi started to call Dave Dubois six times on Sunday. But each time she pulled out his card, her heart started racing, her palms started sweating and she could hardly see the keys on her phone, let alone press them in the right order. She could hardly remember anything about him now she came to think about it, other than his dusty top hat and crazy make-up. Eve was probably right. She was mad to think he might help her make a career in music. *You'll never be a singing star,* she told herself. Reality didn't allow for dreams like that to come true. She had more than enough to deal with as it was, with thoughts of her sister Ruth. And Max was breaking her heart every time she saw him with Eve. And her dad's ongoing misery, and her mum . . .

Rhi didn't want to think about her mum. Every time they saw each other these days – which wasn't often, as her mum seemed to work more hours than ever – they seemed to fight: about school, about Max, about school again. School was her mother's favourite subject.

"No pain, no gain," her mum was fond of saying. And, "Fail to prepare, prepare to fail." Each time she heard those phrases, Rhi wanted to scream.

By the time the cold light filtered through her curtains on Monday morning, Rhi had almost convinced herself the whole weekend had been a dream. It was back to reality now. School, and homework, and long serious consideration of a realist career.

After a shower, Rhi pulled on her uniform, tightened her tie, straightened her skirt and tried to make her unruly hair lie flat and neat beneath her hairclips. She put a dab of mascara on because it was the only bit of make-up her mum wouldn't notice. Ruth had got away with loads of make-up at school in London, she remembered. Lipgloss, mascara, blusher. Things were different now.

She was about to go downstairs for breakfast when

she paused. Ruth's guitar was looking at her, begging to be played. She sat down on the edge of her bed and carefully picked it up, strumming a few chords, trying to keep her hand loose so the strings would sing the way they had for Brody on Saturday night.

She put the guitar down abruptly. It felt as if Ruth was looking at her.

Crossing her room, Rhi picked up the photo from her dressing table. It showed her and Ruth with their mum and dad, laughing into the camera as they posed by the fountains in Trafalgar Square. They had asked a passing police officer to take it, Rhi remembered. A pigeon had landed on her dad's head shortly before the police officer had snapped the picture – that was why they were all in fits of giggles. She could remember it as if it were yesterday. The smell of popcorn, the sound of the fountains and the passing London traffic, the great black lions at the foot of Nelson's Column watching over them.

Ruth and her boyfriend had been killed by a drunk driver two days later. It was the last picture of the whole family that they had.

Rhi sank on to her bed, holding the photograph

tightly in her hand. Although she could remember the day the picture had been taken, she could hardly remember a single day before it. It felt as if her whole life had been spent grieving for her sister. Her family had been broken into pieces that day. They hadn't recovered yet. Rhi wondered if they ever would.

Putting the photograph down again, she caught sight of her face in the mirror. Her eyes had sparkled at the wedding after she had sung. Now they just looked burned out.

Rhi sighed. It was tough, being the only child in a two-child family. She did her best, but it never felt like it was enough.

As she headed downstairs to the kitchen, Rhi tried to focus on what she would need for school. Her dad was leaning over the hob cooking bacon. Rhi could tell from the hunch of his shoulders that he was already having a bad day.

"Hey," she said, hovering at the door.

Her dad's shoulders seemed to loosen. "Hey yourself," he said, looking round at her. "You have time for a bacon sandwich?"

Rhi's mouth watered. "Sure."

She perched at the breakfast bar as her dad flipped the bacon.

"I feel like I haven't seen you in days," he commented as the bacon sizzled. "How was your weekend?"

Rhi wondered where to start. "I did a zombie wedding for Mr Gupta."

"If I didn't know Heartside Bay's habit of weird weddings," said her dad wryly, "I would ask more. I'm sure you'll find the money useful."

"I'll save it for university," Rhi said automatically. It was what her mum was always telling her to do.

"Save it, spend it," said her dad. "It's your money. You earned it."

Rhi couldn't help it. The memories of the weekend were bursting out of her. She had to talk to someone about it.

"Has Mum gone to work already?" she checked a little nervously.

"Don't think so," said her dad. "I haven't heard the car."

Rhi's mother had a habit of popping up unexpectedly. If she was going to tell her dad about the weekend, she had to do it now.

"I sang," she blurted out. "At the wedding. The wedding singer couldn't make it so I did it. I made an extra fifty pounds. And this guy gave me his card and said he was a talent scout and I think I'm going to call him. You know, maybe."

Her dad looked impressed. "You got up in front of a room full of zombies and sang?"

"And I sang at the Heartbeat on Saturday night too," Rhi rushed on. "I did a duet. It was Eve's idea."

"I thought you weren't talking to Eve."

"She didn't think I'd do it. But I did. I did a duet with . . ." Rhi paused, unsure how to describe Brody without making it sound weird. ". . . someone," she finished a little lamely.

"That's great," said her dad, serving up two rashers of bacon on a slice of granary bread. The warmth in his voice was genuine. "Really great."

Rhi picked up the bacon sandwich and prepared to bite into it.

"Oh no you don't."

Appearing from nowhere, Rhi's mother plucked the sandwich from Rhi's hands. She looked extra harried today, in a black suit and crumpled grey shirt.

"Mum!" said Rhi in dismay. "I was—"

Her mother thrust a banana into her daughter's empty hands. "Eat that instead. It's full of potassium, zinc . . . all the things you need to help you concentrate in school." She swept her eyes over Rhi, who wriggled uncomfortably beneath her steely gaze. "You need to lose weight, Rhi. Maybe if you'd lost a stone you wouldn't have lost Max."

Rhi gaped. "What? That's—"

"Max Holmes is a bright boy," said her mother, wagging a finger. "That boy is going places. And now he's going places without you."

"Mum, *he* messed *me* around!" Rhi managed to say.

Her mother looked unimpressed. "You're a silly girl to have lost him. And I hope you were being careful with Ruth's guitar upstairs. I heard you playing it."

It's mine now, Rhi wanted to say. She limited herself to a nod.

"What were you two talking about so intently?" her mother went on, lifting an apple from the fruit bowl.

Don't tell her, Dad, Rhi implored silently. The last

thing she needed today was her mother pouring cold water on her magical weekend.

"Breakfast?" her dad fudged, waving a rasher of crispy bacon at Rhi's mum.

"For heaven's sake, you know I don't eat processed meat, Patrick. And don't change the subject."

"I'm not changing the subject," Rhi's dad said. "I'm just offering you some breakfast."

Rhi's mother looked hurt. "I don't like it when this family keeps secrets."

A dark cloud descended on the kitchen. Ruth's fatal last date with her boyfriend had been a secret. The first they had known of it was when two grave-faced police officers had rung the doorbell.

"It was about the weekend," Rhi's dad blurted into the nasty silence as Rhi wrenched her thoughts from that dark and terrible night. "Rhi sang at the wedding and made some extra money. And she sang at the Heartbeat Café too, in front of her friends. It sounds like she was a hit."

Rhi's shoulders slumped. She didn't blame her dad. Her mum was tough to hide things from. But she could have done without this today.

"I hope they paid you," said her mother.

"I made an extra fifty pounds at the wedding," Rhi mumbled, staring at her banana. She was grateful that her dad hadn't mentioned the talent scout.

Her mother was typically brisk. "That sounds like a useful one-off, Rhi. Enjoy your singing while you can. There isn't long to go now until the real work begins. You have GCSEs just round the corner—"

"They're next year, Mum," said Rhi.

"Like I say, they're just round the corner," her mother said with a little more force. Her eyes flickered over Rhi's dad as she spoke. "Work hard and then you will find a *real* job. The kind that offers security, career progression and a reliable future. I can't stress enough how important that is."

Rhi flinched. Her mother had been making subtle digs about jobs at her dad for years. In her mother's eyes, working in a local art gallery didn't count. The fact that Rhi's dad was trying to follow his dreams had nothing to do with real life. He was supposed to be a doctor, like his wife. Or a lawyer. Anything but a dreamy-eyed painter. When Ruth had been alive, their differences hadn't seemed to matter so much.

Sometimes Rhi wondered why her parents were even together any more.

Another thing I have to make up for, she thought.

She looked at the way her dad was bending silently over the frying pan, scrubbing it with a lump of wire wool. Anger rushed through her.

"I have to go," she said, grabbing her bag before she said something she would regret.

"Be good," her mother called after her. "Make us proud."

You mean, make us feel that having just one daughter isn't so bad, Rhi thought bitterly, slamming the front door and stomping down the road. *Why do I have to be Ruth as well as Rhi? Why can't I just be myself? Ruth was the academic one. I just want to sing.*

Her mother may have been right about why she had lost Max. But she wouldn't let her steal her dreams of a life in music.

In a fit of bravery, Rhi pulled out her phone and stared at the scout's number. She would call him. Right now.

SIX

Rhi pressed dial before she could change her mind. The three rings that followed felt like the longest of her life.

"Yup?"

"Oh, hi," Rhi stuttered, clutching her phone so tightly her knuckles ached. "It's Rhiannon Wills here. We spoke at the wedding on Friday?"

"We did?"

Rhi fought the urge to hang up before she made a total idiot of herself. "I was the singer? You gave me your card, and you said to ring so I thought I. . ."

She tailed off. What was she doing? She was a schoolgirl. This whole idea was stupid!

Dave Dubois's voice changed. "Rhi? The way you

said Rhiannon confused me. That's so great that you called!"

Rhi started to relax. "It . . . it is?"

"Totally. You have an awesome sound. There's so much we could do together."

Despite the wind, Rhi felt warm from her head to her toes. He remembered her! What's more, he sounded like he had genuinely liked her voice. "Great!" she said happily. "So . . . what happens now?"

"Drop by my office any time."

"I'm still at school," Rhi said. Suddenly hoping he wouldn't dismiss her as a dumb schoolkid, she added hastily, "But I can come over straight afterwards?"

"Perfect! Bring your demo tape and we can start making plans."

Rhi faltered. Demo tape? "I . . . that's great," she said, suddenly feeling horrible. "I'll come over soon. Definitely."

"Promise?"

Rhi blinked back the tears. "Sure. Soon. Thanks."

"No, Rhi, thank *you*."

Rhi slowly pocketed her phone as he rang off. Her dreams were in pieces all over again. How could she have been so stupid not to realize that a guy like Dave Dubois would need a demo? She didn't have a demo or any idea of how to get one. She didn't even know anyone she could ask. She certainly couldn't ask her mum for help.

She dragged herself up the steps into school, feeling like she had just been flattened by something heavy. A whole day of lessons was the last thing she felt like right now.

Lila and Ollie were wrapped around each other in reception, kissing. Rhi felt relieved. It had been unsettling to see them being so snippy with each other at the Heartbeat Café on Saturday.

Lila broke away from Ollie's arms and beamed at Rhi. "How's the singing star today?"

There was no point in offloading her unhappiness, Rhi thought. "I've been better," she said with a shrug. "But hey, it's Monday. Everyone feels terrible on Mondays, right?"

"You were awesome on Saturday, you know," said Ollie.

Rhi blushed, feeling pleased. "Thanks, Ollie."

"Incredible," Lila agreed.

"Time to get to class," warned the receptionist.

Lila pushed Ollie down the corridor in front of her. Rhi adjusted the strap on her bag and prepared to follow. She froze as she saw Eve and Max pushing through the double doors. They were arm in arm, Eve laughing at something Max had just said. It was too late to escape.

"Hey, Rhi," Max called, spotting her. "Am I allowed to talk to the Heartbeat's superstar today?"

Rhi really didn't want to talk to Max right now, and certainly not with Eve hanging on to his arm. But there was no escape.

"If you want," she said cautiously.

Max's smile was blinding. "Of course I want. You were incredible on Saturday. Spellbinding. The way you sang that duet blew me away."

"Brody should get the praise," Rhi said, thawing reluctantly. It was hard to stay mad at Max when he smiled at her like that. "He's the one that made the harmonies work. I just sang the tune."

"You did more than that," said Max, shaking his head. "You set the whole room on fire."

There was an intensity in his dark eyes that Rhi

hadn't seen for a while. She was scared by her own response. Max only had to crook his little finger and she would come running, she thought a little hopelessly. She was so pathetic.

"Thanks," she mumbled. She could feel her cheeks flushing. "That means a lot."

Eve tugged Max's arm. "We're going to be late for class," she said loudly. "Oh, hey, Rhi," she added as if she'd only just seen Rhi standing there. "Nice work on Saturday. Unique as ever."

Rhi didn't much like the way Eve said "unique", like it was a bad thing. "I do my best," she said a little coolly.

"That's true," Eve smirked. "No one can say you don't try."

Max looked uncomfortable, but he didn't defend Rhi from Eve's obvious attack.

As Rhi stood there, she realized something. Performing on stage had made her see that she was braver than she thought. She didn't have to stand here and let Eve make her feel worthless. She *could* fight back.

"I think I did a little better than just trying," she said quietly. "The talent scout who gave me his card seemed to think so, anyway."

Eve looked disbelieving. "It was probably just a scam. Nothing will ever come of it."

Perhaps it was Dave Dubois's card in her pocket giving her strength, but Rhi didn't flinch. "Actually, he's already asked me for a demo tape," she said recklessly. She still had no idea how she was going to put a demo tape together, but it sounded good to say it out loud. Like she could make it happen just by speaking the words.

Eve wasn't beaten yet. "Nice dream. It's a shame recording studios are so expensive to hire," she said with a dismissive laugh. "I hope your parents give you a decent allowance."

After two years of being best friends, Eve knew perfectly well that Rhi's allowance was far from generous. But Rhi was determined not to give in.

"I'll work it out," she said, holding her former friend's gaze.

The mockery in Eve's eyes faded. "You're serious, aren't you?"

"I've never been more serious in my life," Rhi answered truthfully.

Eve lifted a shoulder. "Good luck with that, then,"

she said. She turned to Max, brushing something fussily off his shoulder. "Come on, you dope. We're going to be late."

"Wait," Max began, looking at Rhi again.

But Eve dragged him away down the corridor like a dog on a lead. Watching them go, Rhi felt breathless, like she had been running a race. A race that she had, maybe, just won.

The feeling didn't last. When Eve and Max were out of sight, Rhi could feel her whole body sag. How could she have been on top of the world this weekend and fallen to the lowest pits of despair before school had even started on Monday?

She shouldn't have mentioned the demo. All she'd done was give Eve a weapon to tease her with. *How's the demo tape coming along, Rhi? How many songs have you recorded then?* Rhi had a nasty feeling that Eve was right about recording studios. It would be far too expensive to hire one.

She trudged towards her class, keeping her head down. A few people in the corridors congratulated her on her performance on Saturday, but she ignored them. She wished they weren't being so nice. It made it even harder to let go of what was clearly an impossible dream.

Her phone buzzed. Rhi pulled it out of her pocket.

Need help with your demo?

She stared at the name at the top of the screen. Max. *Max was offering to help her.*

After a moment of thought, she tapped out a hasty reply.

Yeah, any ideas?

His response was immediate.

Come to mine after school? You bring the music. I'll figure out the recording studio bit.

Rhi felt giddy. Max was asking her over?

Another message flicked up.

Don't tell Eve ;-)

SEVEN

It was stupid, feeling this nervous. Rhi had been to Max's house a hundred times. She'd stood on this doorstep and stared at the heavy, modern front door the very first time Max had brought her here. Max had kissed her, hard, right here on the doormat. Memories flooded through her. How was she going to cope with spending a whole evening alone with her ex-boyfriend? Was she mad to come here tonight?

This is about the demo, she reminded herself. She adjusted the guitar case on her back. It had been touch and go whether to bring the guitar tonight. Just feeling its weight on her shoulders made her sick with nerves. But she'd written some of her best songs with it. She needed it if she was going to put something together tonight that would really wow the talent scout.

Rhi straightened her tunic and fluffed her hair a bit, then stared at her feet, trying to work up the courage to ring the bell. She realized she was wearing the boots Max always said he liked. Was that why she'd chosen to wear them tonight? To remind him of what he was missing?

Coming here really wasn't a good idea.

Rhi lifted her hand and pressed the bell, listening to the way it echoed through the house. Everything in Max's house was modern and sleek: concrete and glass and wood.

And then the door opened and Max was there. He looked her up and down.

"Hi. Nice boots," he said, cocking his head to one side.

"Can I come in?" Rhi said, trying her best to sound cool.

Max eyed the guitar in surprise. "You play too?"

Rhi nodded shyly. "Kind of."

Max shook his head. "You're a dark horse, you know that, Rhi?" He pulled the door back a little further. "Come on in."

It was strange being back here. Rhi stood for a moment in the impressive hallway, staring at the modern art on the walls.

"You remember where my room is, right?" Max said, halfway up the stairs.

"Sorry," said Rhi a little hurriedly. This was feeling weirder and weirder.

True to his word, Max had set up a makeshift recording studio in his room. Rhi rested the guitar against one white wall, feeling shy, as he plugged the mic into the computer.

"What do you want to start with?" he asked.

"Why are you doing this?" Rhi wanted to understand. It wasn't in Max's nature to do people favours.

He rubbed the back of his head with one hand, the way he always did when he was thinking. "You were good, Rhi," he said at last. "In the Heartbeat. I had no idea you sang like that." He looked at her curiously. "How come you never told me?"

"It's always been a private thing," said Rhi.

"Lila and Polly knew," he pointed out.

Rhi walked around Max's familiar room, studying

the books on his shelves, trying not to show how nervous she was feeling. "I guess girls talk more than boys."

Max nodded, accepting this. He plugged one more lead into the computer. "All set," he said. "There should be good acoustics in here. What do you want to sing first?"

Rhi was feeling increasingly anxious about this whole thing. Did she really want to sing in front of Max, the boy who broke her heart? Singing made her feel extra vulnerable. He'd hurt her so badly.

"How about 'I Wanna Be Like You'?" she joked, making feeble jazz hands. She and Max had watched *The Jungle Book* together once and she knew it was one of his favourite movies, though he would never admit it. Rhi made her voice sound extra-husky as she started to sing and even did a few monkey actions with her arms.

Max was making funny monkey faces at her and singing along. So Rhi kept going.

At some point halfway through the chorus, she realized that Max had stopped singing and was watching her instead. She stopped too, feeling self-conscious all over again.

"Stop staring," she whispered.

"Sorry." He gave her a lazy smile which said he wasn't sorry at all. "I don't often have beautiful orangutans dancing round my room."

He called me beautiful, thought Rhi.

The air thickened as she stared at him. He gazed right back. His face was so familiar to Rhi that she could have drawn him with her eyes closed. Sharp cheekbones, chocolate eyes, hair even thicker and darker than her own. She remembered his lips and the way they had once felt on hers. *Don't think about his mouth*. The ghost of Eve flickered across the room.

"There's nothing to be nervous about," Max said, breaking the silence. "It's just you and me."

That's what I'm nervous about, Rhi thought. "And the microphone," she pointed out.

"Forget the microphone. This is your chance, Rhi," he said seriously. "Your shot at the big time. Get back to being the person who sang at the Heartbeat. The person who—"

He stopped, and fiddled with the computer settings. Rhi wondered what he had been about to say.

"What do you want to start with?" he said, looking up. "For real this time?"

Rhi eyed Ruth's guitar. It was now or never. She unzipped it and stroked it once for luck, then slung the strap round her neck. Her fingers felt like lead. What was she going to sing?

She started with a couple of safe ones that she'd written herself: a ballad called "Way Down Low" and a rockier number called "Sundown, Sunshine". Max listened, fiddled with buttons on his computer, nodding and tapping his foot. "Sundown, Sunshine" needed a couple of takes to get a tricky key change right, but Max just reset the computer and counted her in again.

"It's sounding really good," Max said approvingly as Rhi took a drink of water from a glass on his desk. "One more track should do it. These guys never want more than three."

Rhi swallowed. There was one more song she could sing. The inspiration was sitting right in front of her. Did she dare?

Do it, she thought recklessly. It would be good for Max to hear it.

"I have one called 'Heartbreaker'," she said, keeping her voice as steady as she could.

She thought Max's eyes flickered a little. "Give it all you've got, OK?" Holding up his hand, he folded his fingers away one at a time. "Five, four, three. . ."

Rhi closed her eyes and bent her head. She let her fingers relax, finding the strings. *It's just you and the song*, she told herself. *Nothing else matters. Not Max, not the microphone.*

"Heartbreaker," she sang, her fingers plucking sad sweetness from Ruth's guitar. "Lead me astray. . . Heartbreaker, show me a way. . . Away from sorrow, away from grief, away from pain beyond belief. . . Let me go, make me stay. . . Heartbreaker, show me a way."

The tune was simple and waltz-like. Rhi had poured her heart into it, in those bleak days after she had first discovered Max and Eve together. It was the best thing she'd ever written.

"Back in the days, back in our haze, we talked, we sang, we ran though a maze of feelings," she sang, concentrating on the key changes that would make this part of the song ring out like bells. "No check on time, kisses sublime, we loved, we shared, I cared, I cared without knowing . . . without knowing. . ." Her fingers moved automatically now, back to the opening lilt of notes. "Heartbreaker, let me go, make me stay . . . show me a way."

Dimly Rhi heard a little *plunk* after the last chord of the song. A tear had rolled off the end of her nose and landed on a guitar string. She took the guitar off, set it gently on the floor and scrubbed at her cheeks with both hands.

Suddenly Max was kneeling beside her, his hand on hers. "Don't cry. Rhi, please . . . I'm so sorry . . . for all of it. . ."

Rhi didn't know how it happened, but her arms were round his neck, and his fingers were twisting through her hair, and he was kissing her hungrily and passionately. She could hardly think for the sound of roaring in her ears as she kissed him back. They fitted together so perfectly, lips on lips, arms pulling each other closer. Rhi wanted it to go on for ever. . .

Eve.

Rhi wrenched herself away with a superhuman effort.

"Rhi, I've missed you," said Max. He reached for her again. "You've missed me too, I can tell. Can't we—"

"No!" Rhi was breathing hard. "I won't. We can't do this, Max. You're going out with Eve now, and—"

He tried to put his arms around her again. "But I'm crazy about you. You're amazing. Eve doesn't have to know. You didn't tell her about tonight. I didn't tell her either. So—"

Rhi was trembling all over. "I don't want to hear it! You and Eve may have gone behind my back, but that doesn't make it OK. It's as far from OK as it's possible to be. I'm not a cheat." She took a deep breath. "You can't have us both, Max. You have to choose.

"It's her or me."

EIGHT

Why had she kissed Max on Monday night? Rhi thought gloomily. She had ruined everything.

After she had left his house that night, walking blindly through the dark and clutching Ruth's guitar like some kind of lifeline, Rhi had got home, locked her bedroom door and cried her eyes out. Then she had played "Heartbreaker" again, and cried some more. It was only when she ran out of tissues that she put the guitar away in its case, washed her face and tried to settle down to some homework. She hadn't got much done. Lightning stabs of memory kept distracting her, Max's kiss searing through complicated bits of algebra and French vocabulary. She had never been kissed like that, not even when she and Max had first started going out. What did it mean?

It meant nothing, she thought hopelessly.

The truth was that Max had let her leave. She had wanted so badly for him to tell her that he would end it with Eve, but he hadn't. So Rhi had left. She'd successfully avoided Max and Eve all of yesterday and most of today. And now here she was, heading for the lunch queue on Wednesday, her eyes firmly on the tiled floor in case she saw them together in the corridors and blushed bright red. *How do people cheat and not get found out?* she wondered distractedly. *My face gives everything away.*

"Rhi, wait!"

Lila and Polly were heading towards her.

"Hey, stranger," said Lila, linking arms. Her wide blue eyes were quizzical. "What's up?"

On Rhi's other side, Polly brushed her shiny blue-black hair behind her ears and added: "You look sad."

Rhi felt a rush of anxiety. Did they know already? How had they found out? Had Max been talking? "I don't know what you mean," she fudged.

"Dreaming in class?" Polly prompted, raising her eyebrows. "Ms Andrews asked you that question about Mussolini twice before you heard her. That's not like you."

"Is it about the scout?" Lila asked. "Did you call him? Does he want to hear you again?"

Rhi rubbed her forehead. "It's a mixture of things," she said finally. "I called the scout on Monday."

Lila squealed with excitement. Polly dug her in the ribs.

"And. . .?"

"He wants a demo," Rhi mumbled. Her face was reddening by the minute. "So I made one. Three songs. Max recorded it for me. At least, I think he did. . ." She trailed off miserably. She didn't even know whether Max's recording had worked.

Lila's gaze was suddenly very intent. "*Max* recorded you? Does Eve know?"

Rhi shook her head. "We were at his house and he had the mic all wired up to his computer and . . . I'm so confused," she blurted.

"Uh-oh," said Polly. "Why do I think I know what's coming?"

"Rhi, don't tell me you kissed him," said Lila in dismay.

Rhi bit her lip. She gave a tiny nod.

Polly clapped her hands to her face in shock. "Are you mad? He cheated on you! With your best friend! What were you *thinking*?"

It was such a relief to tell someone, Rhi realized. "I wasn't thinking," she confessed. "That's the point. I sang my last song – it was one I wrote after we broke up. Max made the first move. . ." She trailed off. Her lips were still tingling from that extraordinary kiss. It had to mean *something*.

"I don't like the look in your eyes," Lila groaned. "Rhi, Max Holmes is a cheat. You're not thinking of going out with him again, are you?"

"What's Eve going to say?" Polly's eyes were wide and troubled. "You're poking your fingers into a wasps' nest, Rhi. You know what she's like!"

"I told him he had to choose between me and Eve," Rhi whispered.

"And?"

"He hasn't given me an answer yet."

"Don't do it," Polly implored.

"Polly's right." Lila gave Rhi's arm a little shake. "You're just opening yourself up to more hurt."

Rhi stared at her friends, willing them to understand. "But I love him," she said. "I want to be with him."

"Oh boy," Polly sighed. "I've gone right off the idea of lunch."

Rhi wished they could be happy for her. "It could work out," she said hopefully. "He said he missed me."

Lila and Polly just looked at her with concern. Rhi stared back, feeling defiant. *It's my life,* she wanted to say. *If I want to get back together with Max, that's for me to decide. Not you.*

"Please be happy for me," she said.

Her phone vibrated. Digging it out of her pocket, Rhi's heart jumped in anticipation. It was from Max.

I have the demo.

Usual place in 5?

xx

He'd done the tape, just as he'd said he would. He must care for her to do that, even after the way she had left him on Monday night. And two kisses at the bottom. . . Rhi's stomach fluttered as she read the message again. Their usual place had been by the drama department. They had met there whenever they wanted privacy. He was coming back to her. She knew it.

"See?" she insisted, thrusting her phone under the others' noses. "It's him. He's done my tape. See you later!"

"Aren't you having any lunch?" Lila called as Rhi hurried away with her heart pounding.

"Later!" Rhi called back. Her appetite had gone. All she could think about was Max. She would see him in five minutes. They would be alone.

Rhi suddenly stopped short, and checked behind her. She was probably being paranoid, but she didn't want anyone following her. Especially not Eve.

Max must have broken it off with Eve by now, she reasoned with herself, heading briskly down the corridor. But she checked over her shoulder again, just in case.

She reached the drama department's props room. As she paused against the wall, checking once more that she hadn't been followed, a hand appeared around the door and pulled her inside.

"Hello, beautiful," said Max, gazing down at her with a broad smile on his face.

Rhi fell gladly into his arms. They kissed like they had been apart for weeks, not days.

"I'm so glad you texted," Rhi gasped, breaking off. She could feel her eyes shining in the dark. "I've missed you so much."

He stroked her cheek. "I've missed you too. But at least I had this to listen to."

He waved a CD under her nose. Rhi snatched it from him in delight. *Rhiannon Wills*, she read on the cover. Her demo!

"That last song killed me every time I listened to it," Max confessed. "And I've listened to it a lot. Your scout is going to snatch you up in a second when he hears it."

Rhi felt delirious with everything that was happening. She was holding her first demo, a talent scout was waiting for her call, and she was in the arms of the boy she loved.

Max held her face between his hands and kissed her tenderly. "I'll drop by your house later, OK?" he said against her lips. "I can't stand being away from you."

"How did Eve take it?" Rhi asked against his warm shoulder, snuggling up against him. "Was it awful? Did she go mad?"

Max looked at her strangely. "About what?"

Rhi felt the first fingers of unease. "About us. You did break it off with her, didn't you?"

"Rhi," Max said patiently, "you know I can't break up with Eve. She'd make our lives a complete misery."

"So," Rhi said, trying to make sense of what Max was telling her, "you *haven't* broken up with her?"

He kissed the end of her nose. "You of all people know what she's like. I'm seeing her later, for dinner. I couldn't cancel it. But that doesn't mean I can't stop by yours afterwards."

Rhi couldn't believe what she was hearing. Why hadn't she listened to Polly and Lila? She'd been an idiot to come here! Hadn't she learned *anything*?

She shoved Max backwards so hard that he stumbled into a shelf. Several odd props clattered to the floor – a bowler hat, a walking stick, a police whistle.

"Oh yes it does," she hissed. "Don't come near me again, Max. I mean it!"

Max pulled himself upright, rubbing his head. "Rhi—"

But Rhi had already stormed away, tears of anger clouding her eyes.

NINE

Rhi fixed her red eyes in the girls'-toilets mirror as best she could. Her miserable reflection looked back at her, mocking her.

How stupid are you? Falling for Max all over again.

The only good thing to come out of the whole disaster was the demo tape, sitting snugly in her blazer pocket. The problem was, Rhi didn't feel up to singing to any talent scouts just now. If ever.

Polly put her head round the door. "How are you feeling now, Rhi?"

Rhi listlessly prodded her eyelashes one more time with her mascara wand. "You know," she said with a shrug, pocketing her make-up. "Stupid."

Polly had found her crying by the lockers. Rhi

had told her everything between sniffs, and Polly had listened sympathetically, with the occasional intake of breath and angry shaking of her head.

"You're well rid of him," Polly had concluded, when they had run out of tissues between them. "Listen, why don't you come over for dinner tonight? We can have a good moan about boys and eat my mum's best macaroni cheese."

"Sounds great," Rhi had said gratefully. "Sorry for being so useless."

"You're not useless," Polly had scolded. "You're beautiful, and kind, and you sing like a goddess. You've just had a bad time lately."

Rhi had been too upset to eat any lunch. So right now the thought of macaroni cheese at Polly's house was making her stomach growl. She pinched some colour into her cheeks, tucked her chin deep inside her coat and followed Polly outside.

She didn't say much as they walked. She had too many things to think about. She also kept her head down, afraid of seeing Max or Eve in the crowd. Polly kept glancing at her, checking that she was OK.

"Things will get better, you know." Polly gave

Rhi's arm a squeeze as they walked up the high street together. "You just have to steer clear of Max and focus on your singing. I can't wait to hear the demo. Will you play it for me later?"

Rhi nodded. "But you have to promise you'll be nice about it. I couldn't face any more rejection today."

"If you sound anything like as good as you did at the weekend, I'll be more than nice," Polly promised, grinning. "I'm already a super-fan."

The smell of macaroni cheese was filling Polly's house when they got there.

"Mum!" Polly shouted up the stairs, taking Rhi's coat and hanging it neatly on a peg by the door. "We're back!"

Polly's mother appeared at the top of the stairs, a dressing gown wrapped round her slim body. "Hello, Polly, love. Hello, Rhi." She looked a little flustered. "Can you look after yourselves? I need to leave in ten minutes."

"Where are you going?" Polly called.

But her mother had already disappeared into the bathroom in a fug of scented steam and didn't answer.

"Does your mum usually have baths in the middle of the day?" Rhi asked curiously.

Polly lifted her hands. "Who knows what goes through my mother's mind? I didn't even know she was going out. You want a snack before dinner?"

They sat in the kitchen, munching crisps and drinking juice, jazz playing softly on the radio and the lights on low. Rhi felt relaxed for the first time in days. Polly had a natural calming effect on people, she realized.

Polly's mum burst into the kitchen, checking her watch and smoothing down the red dress she was wearing.

Polly blinked. "Wow," she said.

"There's no need to sound so surprised," said Polly's mum, pulling out a compact and doing her lipstick. "You're not the only one in this house with a great wardrobe, you know."

Polly clearly got her sense of style from her mother, Rhi thought. She looked fantastic. The dress had a vintage look about it, and it fitted her perfectly.

Polly raised her eyebrows. "Do you have a date you're not telling me about?"

Her mother tucked her lipstick into her handbag. "A mother can have a few secrets," she said. "Dinner will be ready in ten minutes. Don't leave the kitchen in a mess, will you? I'll be back later."

There was a jingle of car keys and the front door clicked shut.

"She hasn't dressed up like that in ages," said Polly after a moment. "If I didn't know better, I'd say she was definitely going on a date."

Despite the difficulties at home, Rhi couldn't imagine being cool with the idea of her mum dating someone that wasn't her dad. "Would you be OK with that?" she said cautiously.

"Mum's been single for ages," said Polly. "It would be so great if she found someone nice. But she hasn't seemed interested in anyone since the divorce." She took a thoughtful handful of crisps.

"Was she really hurt when your dad left?" Rhi asked.

Polly's eyes clouded. "We both were."

The macaroni was perfect, crunchy and cheesy and delicious. Rhi gulped it down between sips of juice, and listened to Polly talking about how her dad had settled on a farm in California, and her own plans of visiting him in the summer.

"He's single too," Polly said. She rolled her eyes. "I'm not sure who'd put up with him, to be honest."

"Guys are a lot of trouble," Rhi said.

"Tell me about it!"

Polly spoke with a surprising level of feeling. Rhi blinked. She didn't realise Polly had been having boy problems too. "Is Sam back?" she asked curiously, wondering about the boy Polly had dated briefly at half-term.

Polly coloured, like she'd said more than she had intended. "Not Sam, that's all over. He's in London and probably forgotten about me already. No, it's . . . someone else."

Rhi was intrigued. "Who?"

Polly took a while to help herself to salad. Then she leaned across to Rhi. "Promise not to tell anyone?"

"I promise," said Rhi, and crossed her heart at once.

Polly hid her face in her hands. "I feel really bad about it," she said, her voice muffled. "But I'm kind of . . . OK, more than kind of . . . in love with Ollie."

Rhi gaped. Had she heard right? "Ollie *Wright*?"

Polly peeped through her fingers at Rhi. "I'd never

do anything about it, I swear! He's Lila's boyfriend. But I'm nuts about him. Does that make me an awful person?"

"Of course not!" Rhi exclaimed. "You can't help the way you feel."

"Sometimes I think they're going to break up, and I get all excited, and then I feel even worse," said Polly with a sigh. "Because it's like wishing unhappiness on my best friend, you know?"

"We're in the same situation, aren't we?" said Rhi, realizing. "We both love our friends' boyfriends!"

"Ex-friend, in the case of you and Eve," Polly pointed out.

Rhi giggled. "We're both basically tragic," she said. "Aren't we?"

It felt so nice to laugh.

They cleared up the kitchen and headed to Polly's room. Rhi had been here a few times, but it seemed extra warm and cosy tonight. Perhaps it was because she knew Polly better now they'd shared their deepest secrets.

"Demo," said Polly, holding out her hand.

Rhi's stomach squeezed with anxiety. "It's only

three songs. I wrote the last one when I split up with Max. Even if you hate it, will you promise not to tell me?"

Polly rolled her eyes and plucked the demo from Rhi's hands.

It was weird, hearing herself sing. Rhi hardly recognized her own voice. She sounded . . . well, different to how she imagined. Better or worse? She wasn't sure.

"Heartbreaker," the Rhi on the demo sang quietly, over a ripple of guitar notes. "Make me go, make me stay, show me a way."

There was silence when the song finished. Polly sat very still, staring at her hands. The tension was terrible.

"Tell me, then," Rhi blurted nervously.

Polly lifted her head. "I'll escort you to the talent scout's office after school tomorrow. I will drag you there by your hair if I have to. You have to play it to him, Rhi. It's amazing."

Rhi sagged with relief. "You're not just saying that because I asked you to say that?"

"What will it take for you to believe how good you are?" Polly demanded. She jumped to her feet and went towards her wardrobe. "We're making you an outfit. Right now. You are going to blow this guy's top hat right off his head tomorrow, even if he's not wearing it any more. And that's a promise!"

Thursday seemed to pass in the blink of an eye.

"Why is it," Rhi wondered aloud in terror to Polly in the bathrooms after school, "that when you want time to hurry up, it passes like slow-moving mud, and when you want it to go slowly, it races away?"

Polly handed Rhi a plastic bag. "Hurry up and put this on," she coaxed. They had decided that Rhi would get changed at school to avoid any awkward questions from her mum about the talent scout. Rhi pulled out the green dress that Polly had customized for her.

"You're amazing, you know," she said gratefully. "What you do with clothes is like magic."

"Put it on!" Polly insisted, grinning.

The dress fit Rhi beautifully. Polly had taken a chunk of material off the bottom and finished the new hem with a piece of lace, making it look both pretty and edgy at the same time.

"What about my hair?" Rhi said nervously as Polly

applied eyeliner and glittery eyeshadow to her big dark eyes. "Up or down?"

"Down," Polly said at once. "It's like a beautiful cloud around your face. This guy's going to love you, I promise."

Rhi started feeling a little more relaxed as they headed out of the toilets and down towards reception. Guys were glancing at her, so she figured she looked OK. *It's not the appearance that matters,* she reminded herself. *It's the music.* But she had to admit, she felt really good.

The first dent to her blossoming confidence came when they ran into Eve in reception.

"Aren't you a bit old to be playing fairies?" Eve sounded amused as she ran a practised eye over Rhi's outfit.

Why did Eve always have to be so horrible? What did Max even see in her? Why was he still going out with her? "Polly made it for me. I think it's lovely," Rhi said with as much defiance as she could muster. "We're going to see the talent scout."

For the first time, Eve actually looked interested. "Got your demo done, did you?"

Rhi nodded. *With Max*, she wanted to shout. *We kissed too.*

"You never know," Eve shrugged. "Your talent guy might be the real deal. Although between you and me, that's pretty unlikely. There are a lot of frauds out there. Be careful."

Rhi walked so fast away from school that Polly had to run to keep up with her. Her head was full of thoughts of Max and Eve. She could hardly bear it.

"Eve is vile," she burst out when they reached the bus stop. "I don't know why I was ever friends with her."

"Eve is Eve," said Polly. "Don't let her bother you, Rhi. You have your future to think about right now."

The address on Dave Dubois's card was in a place west of Heartside Bay. Rhi started feeling excited as the bus rumbled down the winding coast road, wondering if the scout had a fabulous recording studio with views of the sea and the cliffs.

The bus dropped them at the bottom of a road of dilapidated flats. Rhi looked around in surprise. Battered-looking cars lined the kerbs, litter blowing among them in the evening wind. A skinny grey cat watched them from a sagging rooftop.

"Are you sure this is right?" she said uneasily.

"Fourteen A, Haig Way." Polly looked at the street sign. "It's up here. Come on."

Rhi felt increasingly uncertain as they walked along the badly lit street. It wasn't how she had imagined at all. They stopped at a communal door with six greying doorbells. Polly pressed the button marked A and they waited on the doorstep, shivering. The wind from the sea was cold.

"Yup?"

"Hi," said Polly, leaning in to the crackly buzzer. "I'm here with Rhi Wills. Is that Mr Dubois?"

"Hey! Come on in, girls. First door on the left."

"Ready?" said Polly, glancing at Rhi as the door clicked open.

Rhi felt inexpressibly glad that Polly was with her. "As I'll ever be," she said bravely.

Dave Dubois' flat was dark, and smelled of cats.

"Sorry about the mess," he said breezily as he let them inside. "I've been all over the place this week. London, New York, Ramsgate. Great to see you, Rhi. You're just as beautiful as I remember."

Polly squeezed Rhi's arm reassuringly. Rhi gulped,

and handed over her demo tape. "Here's my demo, Mr Dubois. I hope you like it."

"I'm sure I will," he said warmly. "Make yourselves comfortable, girls."

Rhi and Polly sat close together on the sagging sofa as Dave Dubois slid the CD into a large stereo in the corner of the room. The ballad tones of "Way Down Low", the rocky beat of "Sundown, Sunshine" and the lilting tones of "Heartbreaker" poured through the room.

When the songs had finished, Dave Dubois whistled. "You are mega-talented, Rhi," he said with a shake of his head. "We're talking the big time here. You could make a fortune with a voice like that. The moment I heard you at that wedding, I knew."

"Knew what?" said Rhi nervously as he sat down on the sofa, a little closer to her than she would have liked.

"That you were going places," Dave Dubois said admiringly.

Rhi knew she should feel excited. Right now, she felt sick.

"So what happens now, Mr Dubois?" said Polly.

He sucked his teeth. "I think we should go the

whole package for you, Rhi. A proper demo, session band, the works. With a little investment, I can get you the record deal of your dreams."

Rhi felt sicker. "What kind of investment?"

"As I said, you want the best," he said. "With a voice like yours, we're looking at something around the ten grand mark."

Ten thousand pounds? Rhi wanted to puke on Dave Dubois' dusty carpet. Where on earth would she get that kind of money?

"That's not how it's supposed to work," Polly said. She sounded just as shocked as Rhi was feeling.

"The music industry is an expensive business," said Dave Dubois sadly. "You want to get someone's attention? You have to pay for it. We could maybe go a little lower if ten's out of your budget. Say, five?"

He had dropped his price by half, and they'd only just started this conversation. Rhi knew in that minute that Dave Dubois was everything Eve had warned her about. Dave Dubois was a fraud.

"I'd like to leave now," she whispered, standing up. Her legs felt wobbly.

"We could try four thousand five hundred," said

Dave Dubois, following Rhi and Polly to the door. "Three? I know this guy with a studio in Heartside who owes me a favour. . ."

Rhi felt stupid. Not only had she fallen for Max again, but she'd fallen for a stupid dream as well. Dave Dubois was no talent scout. She never should have come here.

Grabbing Polly's hand, she dragged her down the dark corridor and out through the big door with its greying doorbells. Somehow now they were both running, past the grey cat and the rusty cars, out towards the streetlight and the bus stop. A bus was already approaching, ready to take them back to Heartside.

Home.

TEN

Friday dawned grey, matching Rhi's mood. Why was everything in her life such a struggle?

Even her mother noticed.

"You need more sleep, Rhi. You can't expect to do your best at school if you stay up late."

"Leave her alone, Anita," said Rhi's dad from behind his paper.

Her mother snapped her bag shut with an irritated sigh. "I'm trying to make sure she stays focused, Patrick. A little support would be nice!"

Rhi's mother left for work in her usual whirl. Rhi kissed her dad gratefully on the top of his head and headed out into the blustery morning. Tears hovered constantly at the corners of her eyes as she made her way to school. How was she going to get through today?

Everyone was too busy to notice how quiet Rhi was. Polly gave her an understanding nod and left her alone. Rhi focused as much energy as she could on her lessons. *This is real*, she thought. *This won't cost my pride and ten thousand pounds.*

At lunch she hung back, taking an extra long time to pack up her bag in history, sharpening pencils and chucking away old biros, so she wouldn't have to walk with the crowd.

"Is everything all right, Rhi?" asked Ms Andrews, walking over to her with a frown.

Startled, Rhi looked up from sorting out her pencil case. "Of course, miss," she said, forcing a smile.

Ms Andrews gave her a shrewd look. "Are you sure?"

Rhi shrugged. Sweeping back her blonde hair, Ms Andrews sighed.

"Well, if there's ever anything you want to talk about, you know where to find me, OK?"

Ms Andrews would be sympathetic, Rhi knew. The history teacher always listened, and looked you right in the eye when you were talking. Not many teachers did that. But where would she even start?

Shouldering her bag, she headed for the lunch hall. She was so engrossed in her thoughts that she almost bumped into someone as she came round a corner.

"Sorry," she said without looking up.

"I'm not," said a familiar voice.

Rhi looked up to see her ex-boyfriend grinning at her. Automatically she looked around for Eve.

"I'm alone," Max said, amused. "There's no need to look so worried."

Rhi flushed. "Go away, Max," she muttered. "I'm not in the mood."

She tried to push past him but he held her back, the smile fading on his face.

"You look upset. What's up?"

"Don't be nice to me," Rhi warned, shaking her head hard.

"Babe, it's me," Max said. "You always used to tell me things. Maybe I can help."

It was no good. Rhi couldn't hold it in any longer.

"I made a mistake with the scout, OK?" she said hopelessly. "It turns out he was a fraud who just wanted money. I feel so angry. And disappointed. And . . . and *dumb*."

Putting her hands to her face, Rhi took a choking, heaving breath. Tears gushed from her eyes, hot and unstoppable.

Max put his arms round her. "Cry all you want, go on," he said, rubbing her back. "Get my shoulder really soaking wet. This blazer could use a few mushrooms to lend it distinction."

Rhi laughed a bit, and then cried some more. It felt so nice, having Max holding her like this, being supportive. *Maybe I shouldn't be so hard on him*, Rhi thought.

"Thanks," she hiccuped, wiping her eyes when the storm of emotion at last began to subside. "I needed that."

When he bent his head towards her, Rhi thought he was going to give her a friendly peck on the cheek. She was so shocked to feel his lips pressing down on hers that, for a moment, she kissed him back. Then reality hit.

She shoved him away. "You're unbelievable," she spat, wiping her mouth. Had anyone seen them?

Max lifted his hands. "I'm sorry! You looked so sad that I couldn't resist."

Rhi hated him so much, she could hardly breathe.

"Just . . . leave me ALONE!" she screamed, before running full pelt down the corridor.

She walked home from school by herself, her coat pulled tight and her arms folded protectively around her waist. She felt like a snail without its shell, soft and vulnerable. If she could just get home. . . If she could just hold it together for another ten minutes. . . Then, maybe, she could start making sense of all the stuff that was happening to her.

As she got nearer to her house, she became aware of the slow, squeaking sound of tyres on tarmac. Was it her imagination, or was a large black car with tinted windows following her? It was going more slowly than the other cars in the road, keeping its distance but never losing sight of her. Rhi shook her head. She had to get a grip on her imagination. It always seemed to get her into trouble.

Unable to help herself, she glanced back at the car as she turned into her road. The car was swinging into the road behind her. Adrenaline surged through Rhi's body. They *were* following her. This wasn't good.

She prepared to break into a run as the car coasted up beside her. A window slid down. Rhi opened her mouth, ready to scream for help.

"There's no need to look like a frightened rabbit, Rhi." Eve swept her red hair away from her face as she leaned one elbow out of the car window. "I'm not going to kidnap you."

Rhi didn't know whether she felt more threatened now, or less. *Eve knows*, she thought wildly. *Someone saw Max kissing me in school today and told her.*

"Actually, scrap that," said Eve. "I *am* going to kidnap you. But I'm hoping you'll come quietly."

"What do you want?" Rhi said in a high, tight voice.

Eve drummed her manicured nails on the car door. "It's something nice, I promise. Get in. Oh, and by the way? I won't take no for an answer."

That was true, Rhi realized. Slowly she moved round to the other side of the car, opened the heavy door and slid into the leather interior beside the person she least wanted to see in the whole entire world.

"You don't do nice things unless there's something

in it for you," Rhi said, mentally preparing herself for a fight. "What do you want?"

Eve studied her nails, letting her hair fall across her face. "You don't have a great impression of me, do you?"

"I have plenty of reasons for that," Rhi retorted.

Eve shrugged. "I guess you do." She leaned forward and tapped on the glass separating her and Rhi from the driver. "Take us to Cliffside, Paulo," she instructed. Checking the little silver watch on her wrist, she added, "And do hurry up. This guy won't wait all afternoon."

Rhi wondered fleetingly if Eve was going to bury her under one of her dad's construction projects. She sat tensely on the leather seat and gazed out of the window. Maybe she should text Polly to let her know she was in trouble.

Eve spent the journey texting, her manicured nails flashing up and down the neat little screen on her smartphone. The black car cruised through a part of Heartside Bay Rhi had never seen before. Huge cliffs towered over them on the right, and the sea was directly to their left.

Eventually the car drew up in front of a

magnificent beach house. Rhi stared at the neatly painted clapboard walls, the clipped topiary hedges, the decking that looped the whole way around the building. A grand white gate at the back of the house opened right on to the beach, with a footpath snaking through whispering marram grass towards the white sand and the sea.

"Finally," Eve said with a roll of her eyes. "I thought we'd never get here. Wait, will you, Paulo? We'll be about half an hour."

Rhi got slowly out of the car. "What is this place?" she asked cautiously.

Eve opened her arms. "Surprise! Max has told me everything."

Rhi felt the colour drain from her face. This was it. The end.

"Max has told you . . . what, exactly?" she whispered.

Eve wagged a finger. "What did I tell you about nasty little men coming up to you at weddings with business cards? Of course he was a fraud. I smelled that one a mile off." She nodded at the beach house. "*This* guy is the real thing."

It was a few moment before Rhi managed to calm

her racing heart. She stared at the extraordinary house, as different from Dave Dubois's cat-smelling flat as it was possible to be. "A scout lives here?"

"Not a scout," Eve said, heading towards the grand front door. "The best producer in the business. He's a business acquaintance of Dad's. I pulled some strings and put in a call and he said he'd see you today." She checked her watch again and tutted. "But we are seriously running out of time. Come on."

Rhi felt like all the breath had been punched out of her. "But, why?" she stammered, following Eve up the path.

"Because I wanted to do a good deed, I guess," Eve said, with a lift of one shoulder. "What's the point in having money and influence if I never get to use it to help my friends? And maybe I owe you one after the business with Max," she added, looking about as uncomfortable as Eve ever got. "This way, you can forgive me and things can go back to how they were."

Rhi didn't know what to say. This was overwhelming. "Thank you," she managed.

Eve rang the front doorbell. "Hey," she said

generously. "It's what friends do."

A tall, handsome man in white jeans and an open-necked black shirt stood on the doorstep, raising his eyebrows enquiringly.

"Hello, I'm Eve Somerstown." Eve held out her hand with the assurance of a movie star. Rhi could only marvel at her confidence. "You must be Andy Graves. This is Rhiannon Wills, the girl I told you about on the phone today."

Andy Graves' eyes flickered over Rhi. She felt like she was being assessed like a prize cow. If she'd known she was coming here, she could have dressed up a little. Her school uniform had never felt so terrible as it did right now.

"I don't have long," he said, sounding a little bored as he stood away from the door. "I'm on a conference call in fifteen minutes."

Rhi's throat went dry. This clearly important person was about to give her some of his time. What if she messed it up?

Andy Graves' phone rang as they stepped inside. He pulled a phone from his shirt pocket. "Contracts will be with you nine a.m. Pacific Standard Time," Rhi heard him say. "Half a mil up front sounds right. Do it. Talk later."

Rhi started to feel seriously terrified. Half a mil? Half a million *pounds*? Maybe dollars? And wasn't Pacific Standard Time Los Angeles? This guy made Dave Dubois look like a funfair sideshow.

Andy Graves slid his phone back into his pocket and studied Rhi with intent blue eyes. "You have a good look," he said. "Even in that hideous uniform. Can you sing?"

"She sings really well, Mr Graves," said Eve. "You won't be disappointed."

Andy Graves continued looking at Rhi.

"I . . . think so, yes," Rhi stammered. "I have a demo but I don't have it with me. I wasn't expecting—"

"Come out to the studio, we'll put you in the booth and record you," he interrupted, checking his watch. "And please," he added, "don't sing me any Adele songs. I've heard the real thing."

Eve gave Rhi a gentle shove in the small of her back. Numbly Rhi followed Andy Graves through the bright, sunlit house, and out into the artfully designed beach garden. A large wooden building stood behind the house, glass windows gleaming in the setting sun. Andy Graves opened the door and ushered Rhi inside. She gazed at the mess of fibre-optic cables, the microphones, the sound desk and headphones and gold discs framed on the walls. An acoustic guitar stood propped against one wall in the soundproofed recording booth.

"Mic the right height?" Andy Graves asked. "I'm going to record you. We can take it from there."

If she was going to do this, Rhi decided, she had to do it right. She eyed the guitar. "Could I borrow that?"

She could hardly believe they were her own hands stretching out to receive the acoustic guitar Andy Graves was handing her. She could see Eve through a glass wall, lounging back on a comfortable chair like she sat in famous producers' recording studios every day.

Rhi lifted the cushiony headphones beside the microphone and settled them on her head. *Focus*, she thought as she tuned the guitar. *Your life depends on these next fifteen minutes.*

"Sound check," said Andy Graves, now on the other side of the glass with Eve. "Say something for me, Rhiannon. I need to get the levels right."

Rhi leaned in to the mic. "Um, hi. It's Rhi. My mum only calls me Rhiannon when I'm in trouble."

"Fine. Good. Rhi. Ready when you are."

The guitar felt strange in Rhi's hands. She cleared her throat. "This is a song I wrote called 'Heartbreaker'."

She fluffed the intro. Her fingers felt like sausages.

"Take your time," Andy Graves said in her ears.

Rhi began again, plucking the strings carefully. Her fingers settled into the rhythm. Her emotions poured into the song.

"Heartbreaker, lead me astray. . ."

It was just her and the headphones, the guitar and the words she had written to express her private heartbreak. She wasn't inside a recording studio. She wasn't inside Max's room. She was inside herself.

She was almost surprised as her fingers fell away from the final chord.

"Come back here, will you, Rhi?" said Andy Graves after a moment.

Rhi took off the guitar and set it against the wall. She opened the adjoining door from the recording booth, feeling so nervous she wondered if she was going to be sick.

Eve's face was unreadable as Andy Graves flicked a switch and played the song back, commenting as they went along.

"A bit pitchy there . . . fell off that note . . . not sure that transition worked . . . you need to work harder on your breathing, it's all over the place. . ."

The criticism continued right to the end of the song. Her cheeks stung with humiliation. Rhi had never been so glad to hear the final chord of "Heartbreaker" in her life.

"Thank you for your time, Mr Graves," she mumbled at the shining wooden floorboards under her feet. "I'll go now."

ELEVEN

"Oh, you're not going anywhere," he said. A smile was splitting the producer's face in half.

Rhi blinked. "What?"

"I said," Andy Graves repeated, smiling more broadly, "you're not going anywhere. Hold on a second." He pulled his phone from his pocket and pressed a button. "Susi? Postpone my conference call, will you? Shall we say an hour?"

Eve, normally so unflappable, sat with her eyes fixed on Rhi's face, looking as shocked as Rhi felt.

"You . . . you like me?" Rhi said incredulously.

"I love you." Andy Graves' blue eyes were now as warm as the Caribbean sea. "Your voice needs a little work, but your depth of tone and feeling remind me of some of the greats."

Rhi had never loved her ex-friend as much as she did right at this moment. Eve had made the impossible possible. Impulsively, she threw her arms around the red-haired girl. Eve briefly returned the hug, then pushed Rhi back.

"There's no need to get soppy," she said briskly. But Rhi could see that she was smiling.

Andy Graves opened the door of the recording studio and ushered them out into the darkening garden. "There is a great deal I want to do for you, Rhi," he said, striding towards the house. Rhi and Eve had to run in order to keep up. "You'll need a complete makeover, of course. I know a band that's looking for a new lead singer. You would be the ideal replacement. They have a recording contract in place and are coming down to record in my studio next month. We'll go up to London next week and meet them. . ."

"Next week?" Rhi squeaked.

"That sounds acceptable, Mr Graves," said Eve.

Rhi didn't know how Eve could sound so cool. She was having difficulty keeping her feet on the ground. This was all happening so fast. Lead singer of a band? What *kind* of band?

Andy Graves laughed. "I'm glad to hear it's acceptable. Questions?"

Rhi had so many, it was difficult knowing where to start. She grasped for the question that, to her, felt like the most important one in her head right now.

"Did you like my song?" she said. "Or . . . or just my voice?"

"Your song was adorable." Andy Graves ruffled the top of Rhi's head.

Rhi felt oddly deflated.

"But this band I have in mind are going to be the next big thing, especially with you at the helm," Andy Graves went on. "You could be touring next year. I'll have my assistant call and set up a meeting to discuss contracts as soon as possible. There's no time to waste. The music industry moves fast, young lady. We have to move with it."

The next half hour passed in a whirl of words. Agents, PR, promos, managers, session rates, digital downloads. Rhi sat in a haze on a large white sofa in the brightly lit sitting room, letting it flow over her like water. She couldn't help feeling they were discussing someone she didn't even know.

"Good," said Andy Graves, clapping his hands briskly to indicate, Rhi supposed, that the meeting was over. "I'll have my assistant call and set up a meeting to discuss contracts in more detail. Make sure you leave good contact numbers. I'll be in touch."

Outside, Paulo the driver clicked the passenger door shut behind Rhi and Eve and slid into the driver's seat. As the engine roared into life, Rhi pressed her palms to the car window, watching Andy Graves spotlit by his big beach house with one hand raised in farewell.

They were halfway up the road when Eve suddenly whooped: "My God, Rhi, he *liked* you. Do you have any idea how unusual that is?" She flopped back against the leather seats, looking smug. "I knew I'd done the right thing getting that guy on board. You're going to be famous!"

"This kind of thing doesn't happen to me," Rhi said, shaking her head.

Eve patted her arm. "It does now. Let's go to the Heartbeat and celebrate. I'll let the others know we'll be there in half an hour. They are going to bust a *gut*."

Thanks to some swift texting on Eve's phone, everyone was waiting for them at the Heartbeat. Rhi had barely squeezed through the café door before she was jumped on and hugged half to death by her friends.

"You sneaky thing!" said Lila in delight. "How come you didn't tell anyone you were going to see a real producer?"

"I didn't know," Rhi said, high-fiving Ollie. "Eve did it all."

Eve gave an elegant shrug.

"And he was the real thing?" Polly said, her eyes wide and amazed. "Not another dodgy money-maker like that guy and his smelly cat-flat?"

Rhi hugged Polly tightly. "If his house was anything to go by, he was the real thing all right. You should have seen the size of his living room!"

"Of course he was the real thing," said Eve, rolling her eyes and flopping down at their usual table. "I wouldn't have contacted him otherwise."

"That's fantastic news, Rhi," said Max warmly, coming forward to hug her.

Rhi tried not to stiffen. How was she supposed to

manage her feelings for Max, now that Eve had done this incredible thing for her?

"Celebrating something?"

Ryan had appeared at their table, his notepad poised for orders.

"You could say so," Lila grinned.

Ollie flung an arm round Rhi. "This girl is going to be famous!" he announced.

"Awesome," said Ryan enthusiastically. "Is it your singing, Rhi?"

"Well, it's hardly going to be her tap dancing," Eve drawled.

"Don't be mean, Eve," Lila said with a sigh. "Frappé for me, Ryan. Anyone else?"

Poor Ryan, thought Rhi, as he scribbled down their orders with his fringe over his eyes as usual. Lila only had to speak and he turned as red as a tomato. It was clear that he wanted to hang out and share the gossip, but his dad was calling him back to the bar.

One person was missing from the celebrations, Rhi thought, sitting back on the bench with Polly and Eve on either side of her. It was Friday, though. Maybe he'd be performing later. Maybe he'd come through the door, with his fruit-sticker guitar slung over his shoulder and his bright blue eyes gleaming, ready to wow the weekend crowd. Just now, she felt as if Brody Baxter was the only person who would help her make sense of what was happening to her.

"Ryan?" she called, feeling strangely nervous.

Ryan turned back hopefully.

"Is Brody playing tonight?"

Ryan scratched his ear with his pencil. "Not tonight, no. He's at the Stag's Head down on the coast road."

Rhi was surprised at the strength of her disappointment. *You've only met him once,* she reminded herself. *He's probably forgotten who you are by now*. Why did it feel so important? This was exactly what she had always wanted, wasn't it?

"Hey," said Eve, nudging her. "What's with the faraway look? You're the star tonight, Rhi, not surfer boy."

Rhi thought she saw Max's eyes flicker in annoyance at the mention of Brody Baxter. Refusing to let herself dwell on it, she smiled at Eve instead. "None of this would have happened without you," she said honestly. "I am so grateful. You didn't have to do any of it."

Eve looked pleased. "When I feel like doing something, I do it. I'm just glad it worked out." She squeezed Rhi's arm. "So we're friends again? We can put everything else behind us?"

Eve's smile seemed so hopeful, and her grey eyes so uncharacteristically uncertain, that Rhi felt convulsed with guilt all over again. She had kissed Max twice in the last few days, and enjoyed every lip-tingling moment. She had to move on. *Let Eve have Max,* she told herself. *It's the least you can do.*

"It's great to have you back," she said honestly. "You may have just changed my life."

Eve's eyes blazed with pleasure. "Do you mean that?"

Rhi pulled out her warmest smile. "Of course I mean it, you idiot." And she did. Eve could be difficult sometimes, there was no doubt about it, but she'd always been a good friend – at least until she'd stolen Max. And Rhi realized that she'd been missing her. And now Eve had just given her this incredible opportunity. Thinking about Andy Graves' reaction to her singing made Rhi want to jump on the table and crow like a cockerel. It really was what she'd always wanted, she told herself.

So why did something about it not feel quite right?

TWELVE

It took until breakfast on Saturday for Rhi to work up the nerve to tell her parents about Andy Graves. Her mum was the first to react.

"This man wants *what*?" she said, half-rising from the table. Even on a Saturday, she was dressed as if she were about to go to work.

Rhi poured juice into her glass, trying not to let her hand shake. "He wants to sign me as the lead singer of this band he's got, and he wants a meeting to discuss a contract. I gave him our home number because I'm underage and he needs to speak to you about everything."

"Rhi, be serious," said her mother with a strangled laugh. "You're still at school. You have exams, a future to consider. What kind of person wants a young girl in the middle of a promising academic career to front a pop band?"

The way her mother said "pop" made Rhi wince. "He's a real professional, Mum," she said, desperate for her mother to understand. "He has gold discs on his wall. And this amazing recording studio in his garden, and he was taking a call from LA when Eve and I got to his house. He's genuine, Mum, I know he is."

She wondered whether to mention her and Polly's disastrous trip to see Dave Dubois as proof that she knew what she was talking about, but decided against it.

"Rhi," her mother said in the patient voice she used when she thought Rhi was being particularly stupid, "this whole thing is clearly a scam. Do you know how many young girls throw away everything on silly dreams like this? You are very naive if you believe this man can give you so-called fame and glory."

"I'm not interested in fame and glory," said Rhi as evenly as she could. "I'm interested in making music. Mr Graves can make it happen for me, Mum. Look him up if you don't believe me."

"Well, I think it's fantastic," Rhi's dad announced before Rhi's mother could think of anything else to say. He wrapped Rhi in a bear hug. "You clever girl. What was he like? Does he keep a yacht in Heartside harbour? I bet he does, for all his pop-star parties, eh?"

"That's just typical of you, Patrick," said Rhi's mother with an irritated sigh. "Ever the dreamer."

She pulled out her tablet and started tapping busily on to the screen. Rhi held her breath. The only way her mother would back her in this was if she could see for herself that Andy Graves was everything he said he was.

"Well I can't say I've heard of any of these bands he supposedly produces," said Rhi's mother a little stiffly after a few moments. "But I suppose he *could* be legitimate." She stared at the tablet with a frown on her face, as if willing the pages of information on *Andy Graves, music producer* to disappear in smoke and prove her original suspicions correct.

"So you'll talk to him?" Rhi said hopefully.

"I'll read through the contracts," she conceded. "But if there's even the smallest hint that this man is after more than—"

Rhi rushed round the table to give her mother a hug. "Thank you, oh, thank you!" Her mind whirled with everything she wanted to discuss with her mum. She'd been starting to worry that she was selling out. She wanted to sing her own music, and she wasn't sure about the whole idea of being in a band. . .

Her mother pulled away from the hug, checking her watch. "I have to go. Surgery hours can't wait."

Rhi blinked. "You don't work at the weekends."

"Dr O'Donnell is sick so I said I would do the Saturday clinic." She took up her briefcase. "We'll talk about this later."

"We can't talk about it later," said Rhi a little desperately. "I'm doing another wedding for Mr Gupta, and I need to—"

"Rhi, I'm sorry," said her mother with a sigh, "but I don't have time this morning. Perhaps we can talk about it tomorrow."

This was the biggest thing that had ever happened to Rhi, and her mother was leaving for work like it was just an ordinary day? *I want to talk about it now!* she wanted to shout as the front door banged shut. But it was too late.

"Your mother is very stressed at the moment," said her dad into the awkward silence.

"When isn't she?" Rhi said bitterly.

She stood up from the table and headed for her room. She had to get away from her dad's helpless face. She didn't want to cry today.

At two o'clock, Rhi stood on Polly's doorstep, shivering in the cold wind that was blowing straight in from the sea. No one was answering the door. She checked her watch. Polly had been making Rhi's outfit for the angels-and-devils-themed wedding tonight, and Rhi was meant to be trying it on this afternoon. Polly had definitely said two o'clock, hadn't she?

Suddenly Rhi wasn't sure.

Reaching to press the doorbell again, she noticed that the door was on the latch. She pushed it open and peered inside.

Polly's house was beautifully decorated, pastel colours on the walls and bright, cheerful travel posters hanging in unusual frames down the hallway. It was much warmer inside than out. Rhi stepped through the door, relieved to escape the chill.

There was a flash of movement from the kitchen, straight ahead down the hallway from where Rhi was standing. Rhi caught a glimpse of Polly's mum through the half-closed kitchen door, her head thrown back in laughter. Someone else was in the kitchen with her. From the low murmuring voices, it sounded like a private conversation, and not something Polly's mum would appreciate being overheard.

Rhi suddenly felt like an intruder. She didn't want to go back out into the cold, but she couldn't stay here. Where was Polly? Maybe they'd said three o'clock, not two. Her head was all over the place at the moment. She wouldn't be surprised if she'd got it wrong.

In the kitchen, all sounds of conversation ceased. Rhi realized with horror that Polly's mother was kissing whoever was with her. She needed to leave before she was seen. She shouldn't have come inside in the first place.

She started backing quietly towards the front door again, hoping that no one came out of the kitchen and saw her. Part of her wanted to giggle at the situation.

It was great that Polly's mother had found romance. Polly had said that her mum had been unhappy and lonely since the divorce six years earlier. *At least it's working out for someone,* Rhi thought, doing her best not to remember kissing Max in the drama props cupboard.

As Rhi reached the front door, there was another flash of movement from the kitchen. She paused in surprise as she recognized the person hugging Polly's mother.

It was Ms Andrews.

Rhi had a ridiculous urge to rub her eyes, in case seeing her and Polly's history teacher kissing Polly's mum was a mirage. It wasn't. Ms Andrews' blonde hair was unmistakable, and so was the red jacket she often wore in class.

This was . . . unexpected.

Rhi of course had no problem with the idea of two women kissing each other. But what would Polly make of it? Rhi knew Polly was still pretty fragile about her parents' divorce. She imagined with horrible clarity what the school gossips would say if they found out.

She didn't want to see any more. Turning, she ducked through the front door and out into the cold again, leaving the front door half-open, just as she had found it.

THIRTEEN

"You're quiet, Rhi," Polly remarked, straightening the angel wings on her back. "Is everything OK?"

Rhi had been staring at the devilishly dressed bride and her new husband in his angel toga and gold body paint, and thinking about Polly's mum and Ms Andrews. She gave a guilty start. "What? Yes, everything's fine!" she said quickly. "Sorry, I'm a thousand miles away. I've got a lot to think about."

That was true at least, she thought.

Polly's face lost its worried expression. "Of course!" she said. "Your head must be full of that producer guy. Eve's such a surprise, isn't she? Who'd have thought she had it in her to be so nice?"

"Even Eve has a bit of angel about her," Lila

laughed. She was wearing a short, floaty red dress with a set of flashing devil horns on her head completing the picture.

"This has to be one of the maddest weddings we've done yet," Rhi said, gazing around the angels-and-devils-themed marquee.

Black and white fabric swathed the walls, and red, white and black balloons floated around the pleated ceiling above the guests' heads. Tables were laid with a mixture of red, black and white cloths, topped with huge glass vases filled with blood red gerberas, pure white lilies and deep purple roses. A large open-topped barbecue stood in one corner of the marquee, its coals glowing like a cartoon vision of the underworld, and on a table by the door, white twinkling lights were wound around a pure white wedding cake decorated in sugarcraft feathers. "Sympathy for the Devil" played on the sound system, shortly followed by "There Must Be an Angel (Playing With my Heart)". The DJ, clad half in white and half in black with a painted red face, was having plenty of fun with the theme.

Rhi smoothed the angel dress Polly had made for her, admiring the glimmery ribbons that Polly had stitched along the hem. Her wings were light and glittery on her back.

"I love this dress, Polly," she said gratefully. "I feel properly angelic."

"You'd look angelic even without it," said Polly, smoothing back her newly platinum-blonde hair. The pale shade suited her, making her expressive hazel eyes shine and giving a fresh glow to her skin. She looked fantastic in her floaty white dress and wire-stiffened dragonfly wings.

"Stop admiring yourselves, girls," said Mr Gupta, swerving past in his usual grey suit and tie. "We need the canapés now, please. Circulate! Circulate!"

Rhi obediently scooped up a tray of devils on horseback: small prunes wrapped in bacon. Lila's tray was full of angel cake, and Polly had devil's food cake. As Rhi began to move through the crowd, turning sideways occasionally to fit her wings through the small gaps, she marvelled at the chances of two people ever getting together and finding happiness. This wedding had an original theme for sure, and everyone was enjoying themselves. But how did any marriage last? If there was one thing Rhi had learned, it was that nothing was ever certain. A cheating partner. A secret relationship. A drunk driver.

She felt her phone vibrate in the hidden pocket Polly had stitched into her dress. Hurriedly setting down her tray, Rhi took it out, shielding it from view with her wings. Mr Gupta didn't like them taking personal calls or texts at work.

Missing u superstar xxx

Rhi's heart sped up. It was Max. She typed a swift reply.

Don't text me at work!

A message came straight back.

I bet you look gorgeous right now.
Meet me later? xxx

Rhi closed her eyes. She pictured meeting Max outside in the dark in her beautiful dress, and kissing him. She only allowed herself the thought for a split second.

She wouldn't do it. She couldn't go behind Eve's back, especially now. Squeezing her phone hard, she replied:

I'm not a cheat!

The reply took a moment to pop up.

Meet me. Please.
I miss you so much.
I know I don't deserve you.
xxx

Rhi resisted the urge to reply. She turned her phone off, tucked it away in her angel pocket and picked up her tray again, feeling tears at the backs of her eyelids.

"Hurry, please, Rhi," Mr Gupta snapped, rushing past in the opposite direction. "There is no food in the far corner of the marquee."

Rhi waded back in among the laughing, chattering guests. She smiled, and served, and bit back the urge to sneak into a corner to check her phone one more time. What was she doing? The angels and devils theme was horribly appropriate tonight. It felt like the angels and devils were playing tug of war in her brain.

For all her good intentions, she was wavering about Max. She still loved him. She didn't want to, but she did.

What should I do? she thought in despair.

Her brain answered in a loud, confused clamour.

Be with Max.

Don't hurt Eve.

Be a famous pop star in a band.

Keep writing your own music.

Stay in school and get a normal career.

Tell Polly about her mum and Ms Andrews.

Don't tell Polly about her mum and Ms Andrews. . .

What were the answers to all the terrible dilemmas she was facing?

"Invisible canapés, are they, love?"

Rhi realized she was holding out an empty tray towards a quizzical-looking angel.

"I . . . sorry," she stuttered, suddenly aware of Mr Gupta ploughing through the crowd towards her. "I'll fetch some more."

She fled back towards the catering area. In all her

confusion, one answer shone out clearly. She didn't like it, but at least she knew it was the right thing to do. Putting her empty tray down on the first table she passed, she yanked out her phone and turned it on before she lost her nerve.

As long as you're with Eve we can only be friends.
Take it or leave it.

As soon as she'd sent Max the message, she put her head in her hands and groaned miserably to herself.

How come the right thing felt so hard?

FOURTEEN

"How do I look?" said Polly for the sixteenth time.

"Great," Lila said, hopping from side to side as she yanked on her boots. "You looked great the last time you asked too. Repeat after me: going blonde was a good move. Blonde is really fresh. Now can we go? Everyone will have left the Heartbeat by the time we get there!"

Rhi stroked her angel dress one more time, then folded it and tucked it inside her bag. Her pay packet crinkled in her coat pocket. "I have had enough angels and devils to last me a while," she sighed. "It's hot chocolate all the way from now on."

"I'm so with you," Lila said, licking her lips. "The Heartbeat does the best hot chocolate in town."

"Frothed right to the top, with caramel and chocolate sprinkles," added Polly with a sigh.

"Then what are we waiting for?" said Rhi, smiling.

The Heartbeat Café was a ten-minute walk from the wedding venue. Huddled up against the cold, talking and laughing with her friends, Rhi started feeling a little less confused by all the problems in her life. She decided the answers would come in their own time, and a Heartbeat hot chocolate might even help.

"We thought you'd never get here," Eve moaned as Polly, Rhi and Lila came through the door of the café in a blast of cold air. She was sitting at their usual table with Max and Ollie. "Weekend jobs are *seriously* inconvenient."

"If only I had more money than sense," said Lila, kissing Ollie and flopping down on the bench. "Like you, Eve."

"Whoa," said Ollie, his eyes widening as he took in Polly's new hair. "You look like Marilyn Monroe, Pol."

Rhi could guess how much Ollie's opinion would matter to Polly.

"Thanks," Polly said, bowing. "You look like Marilyn Monroe too."

Ollie put on a breathy voice and started singing "Happy Birthday, Mr President" to general laughter. Rhi put an arm round Eve's faux-fur shoulders, doing her best to avoid Max's eye.

"I'll buy you a hot chocolate to make up for being so late, Eve," she said.

Eve looked mollified. "I suppose I could fit one in," she said, patting her stomach.

No sooner had Lila raised her hand to get a waiter's attention than Ryan was at their table, looking eager and floppy-haired with his notepad in his hand.

"The usual?"

"No frappés," said Lila, tucking her glossy brown hair behind her ears. "We're going hot tonight."

"Right," repeated Ryan, looking at Lila. "Hot."

There was a pause as everyone stared at him. *Oops*, thought Rhi. She had a sudden urge to hide her head in her hands. Did Ryan realize what he'd said?

Ollie glared. "That's my girlfriend you're drooling over, mate."

Ryan blushed and looked back at his notepad.

"Sorry, I didn't mean . . . I was thinking hot, not *hot*, but . . . you know," he fumbled, losing confidence by the moment.

"Smooth," remarked Max, reclining easily with his arm along the top of the bench behind Eve's shoulders as Lila giggled and pulled a face at Rhi. "I bet you're a real hit with the ladies, Ryan."

Eve had started laughing too. Rhi felt so sorry for Ryan that she reached out her hand and touched his sleeve. "Ignore them," she said. "Do you want to join us for a bit?"

Ryan looked at Rhi with a combination of shock and delight. He glanced back at the bar, where his dad was chatting to customers. "I'm supposed to be working, but I guess I could take a little break. . ."

Lila kicked Ollie's shin and made him move up. Ryan squeezed on the end of the bench while Rhi waved a different waiter over to take their orders.

"So," Ryan said, clearing his throat as hot chocolates were delivered to the table. "Everyone OK?"

"We've had more exciting evenings," said Eve pointedly.

Rhi wanted to kick her. Couldn't Eve see how

awkward Ryan was feeling right now? "What's your news then, Ryan?" she said, trying her best to get the conversation going.

"Oh, you know," said Ryan. "Not much. Just the usual gossip."

"Please let it be good," said Eve, rolling her eyes.

Ryan shrugged. "Oh, it's good," he said. "But you've probably heard it already."

Ollie stopped glaring. "Heard what?"

Ryan smiled in delight. "You haven't heard, have you?"

"Spit it out," said Max impatiently.

Ryan steepled his fingers and appeared to be deep in thought. It was clear that he was enjoying the attention. Suddenly Rhi found herself wishing she hadn't invited him to join them at all.

"I've got some dirt on a teacher that'll blow your heads off," Ryan said, smiling coyly around the table.

Lila and Polly looked shocked. Max, Ollie and Eve leaned forward with interest. "Who with?" said Ollie. "Mr Morrison?"

"If this is the one about the PE teacher, the whole school knows about it," said Max.

"Let Ryan speak, would you?" said Eve, drumming her manicured fingers on the table.

Rhi felt cold to her bones. As soon Ryan had mentioned a teacher, she knew what was coming. She shot a glance at Polly, who was quietly holding her hot chocolate, nibbling off the chocolate and caramel sprinkles.

"It's about Ms Andrews," said Ryan exultantly.

Rhi half-rose from the table as the others murmured with surprise and interest. He wouldn't say anything in front of Polly, would he? Rhi didn't want to take that risk. It suddenly felt very important to change the subject.

"Ryan," she said quickly, "could you get us some serviettes? I've spilled my hot chocolate. . ."

Eve patted her arm. "That can wait, babe. This is much more interesting. What about Ms Andrews, Ryan?"

Don't say it! Rhi pleaded silently.

Ryan was clearly stringing this out for maximum effect. "It's pretty juicy," he said, shaking his head. "I don't know if I should say anything. . ."

"You can't start something and not end it," Ollie objected.

"Ask me nicely," smirked Ryan, examining his nails. "If you're nice enough, I'll tell you."

"And if you don't tell us right now," Eve said in a sweet-sounding voice, "we'll make your life a living hell."

"She means it, mate," said Max, sounding amused.

"OK," Ryan said hurriedly. He lowered his voice to a whisper. "*Ms Andrews is having an affair.*"

Rhi felt completely powerless. Make a fuss and everyone would realize something was up. Stay quiet and Polly's life might be in tatters. Here was yet *another* angel and devil to contend with. What could she do?

"Who with?" said Lila, startled.

I'm sorry, Polly, Rhi thought in desperation. *I should have told you first—*

"I don't know," Ryan confessed.

Everyone groaned. Rhi sagged against the bench cushion in relief.

"Call this gossip?" said Eve in disgust. "I get more interesting news from my father."

"I'm telling you everything I know!" Ryan protested, looking annoyed. "She's having an affair

130

with a parent at the school, OK? I overheard her talking to the principal about it."

Eve's gaze sharpened. "Now *that's* a little more interesting. An affair technically means she's seeing a married man."

"Naughty Ms Andrews," said Max with a laugh.

Polly suddenly spoke up. Hearing her voice made Rhi realize she hadn't joined in the conversation at all to this point.

"Leave Ms Andrews alone," she said, setting down her hot chocolate mug. "She's a friend of my mum's and she's lovely. Gossip ruins lives, Ryan. Teachers are allowed as much privacy as the rest of us."

"Hear, hear," said Lila, banging the table.

"Maybe she's seeing your dad, Ryan," said Eve blandly.

Ryan coloured. "Dad wouldn't cheat on Mum!"

Eve spread her hands. "Who knows? Teachers are weird. I mean, who would choose to go *back* to school after *leaving* school? No one sane, that's for sure."

Rhi couldn't stand another moment. She stood up.

"Bathroom," she said abruptly.

Sometimes her friends were so frustrating. How could they be so casual about people's lives? She had lived with rumours and gossip after Ruth had died. As if life hadn't been difficult enough, she'd had to contend with people talking in corners and looking at her all the time with pity in their eyes. She would never inflict that on anyone.

Leaning against the bathroom sinks, she concentrated on calming down. It was killing her, knowing Polly's mother's secret. She had to talk to Polly about it, especially now that the gossipmongers had started their dirty work.

The bathroom door opened.

"Everything OK?" enquired Eve.

"I just needed some space," Rhi sighed. "I can't stand gossip. It's so . . . *ugly*."

Eve folded her arms and leaned against the bathroom wall. "It's just human interest," she said.

"It eats you up," Rhi said passionately. "Knowing people are talking about you behind your back. Not knowing if the next person you see will flicker their eyes at you in that horrible furtive way. I've been there, and believe me – it's bad. It makes a difficult time even more difficult."

Eve nodded. She knew about the problems Rhi had faced when her sister had died. "What's this really about?" she asked curiously.

I need to tell someone, Rhi thought. *Before I burst under pressure.*

"Ms Andrews," she said, rubbing her temples. "When it gets out who she's seeing, it's going to be different. It's a woman. And not just any woman." She looked unhappily at Eve. "It's Polly's mum."

As soon as she'd spoken, Rhi wished that she hadn't. Eve was so unpredictable. How on earth would she react to the juiciest piece of gossip in Heartside High?

"A woman?" Eve's eyes were wide and astonished. "Are you saying . . . are you saying Ms Andrews is gay? And seeing Polly's mum? Does Polly know?"

Unease was crashing over Rhi in waves. She shouldn't have said anything. Especially not to Eve. But the damage was done now. She just hoped it wouldn't backfire.

"Polly doesn't know anything. I saw her mum and Ms Andrews together a few days ago. They didn't see me." She swallowed. "You won't tell anyone I told you?"

Eve smoothed back her hair. "Of course I won't."

Why don't I believe her? Rhi thought. "What do you think I should do?" she blurted.

"Why should you have to *do* anything? It's not up to you to fix everyone's lives, Rhi."

Rhi thought she caught a wobble in the red-haired girl's voice. She dismissed it almost at once. Eve never wobbled at anything.

"You don't think I should warn Polly?" she said hesitantly. "The rumour has started now. I'd hate for Polly to find out that I . . . we . . . knew and didn't say anything."

"You said it yourself." Eve looked more serious than Rhi had ever seen her. "Teachers are entitled to a private life. Even Ms Andrews. Maybe especially Ms Andrews," she added after a moment. "She's one of the decent ones, after all."

Rhi didn't know what to make of this. It was unlike Eve to be so compassionate.

"Stop looking at me like I've grown two heads," said Eve impatiently. "Let's go back to the others or they'll start a rumour about *us*. Plus this bathroom stinks. Cheap air freshener is *such* a short-term solution."

She marched out of the bathroom. After a moment's hesitation, Rhi followed.

FIFTEEN

At school on Monday, Rhi felt hyper-aware of people's conversations. The group of girls hanging around the lockers: were they talking about Ms Andrews? Had someone heard her and Eve talking in the bathroom? The shouts of laughter in the corridors: had someone made a joke about Polly's mum? It was exhausting.

Rhi watched Polly carefully as well. She had been her normal chatty self in English, giggling with Lila and batting off admiring compliments from boys about her new hair colour. Rhi wished she could stop the gossip from breaking over Polly's head. It was bound to, sooner or later. At least, for now, it was looking more like later.

"Lunch?" said Polly as the bell rang, signalling the midday break.

"I'm so hungry I could eat a unicorn burger," announced Lila. "Arrest me now, fairy police."

Rhi quailed at the thought of enduring any potential whispers of the canteen. "You guys go on," she hedged. "I need to, uh, fetch something from my locker."

When Lila and Polly had gone, Rhi wandered over to her locker in the vague hope that there might be a packet of crisps or an apple or something that she could eat. She poked around without much expectation, then locked up and braced herself for the canteen.

Voices were coming from Ms Andrews' class. Rhi slowed as she passed the door, recognizing the hum of both voices. It was Ms Andrews – and *Eve*.

Eve didn't even take her classes. What was going on? What would Eve have to say to Ms Andrews that had to be done in private? It must be about the secret Rhi had sworn Eve to keep. Had she broken her promise already?

The voices were muffled and unclear, but Rhi got the sense that it was a serious conversation. She moved a little closer to the door with her heart in her mouth. There were a few more murmured words, then silence.

The classroom door flew open unexpectedly.

Rhi backed away in a panic, stumbling over her own feet. This was going to look really bad, she knew. But it was too late. Eve was in the doorway, staring at her in what Rhi could only interpret as horror.

Pulling the door tightly shut behind her, Eve took a step towards Rhi. "What were you doing outside the door?"

She looked scared. *I can't back down on this*, Rhi thought. *It's too important.* She stepped even closer to Eve until their noses were almost touching.

"What were *you* talking to Ms Andrews about?"

Eve's eyes darted from side to side, like this was the last conversation in the world that she wanted to have. She looked so guilty that Rhi knew her suspicions were correct.

"I told you about Ms Andrews and Polly's mum in private," she reminded Eve in a trembling voice.

The red-haired girl folded her arms tightly across her body. "I didn't say anything about that."

"Then why are you looking so nervous?"

138

Eve's eyes flashed. She said nothing.

"What were you talking about?" Rhi repeated.

"None of your business."

"If it was about a secret I told you to keep, then it *is* my business, Eve," said Rhi.

Eve leaned back against the corridor wall. "Stay out of it," she said coldly.

Rhi didn't know what to think. She didn't want to fall out with Eve again, but there was something Eve wasn't telling her.

"Hey," said Max, sauntering up the corridor towards them.

On top of all her fears and doubts about Eve's trustworthiness, Rhi couldn't handle Max as well. She abruptly turned to go.

"Wait," said Max, pulling her back and smiling into her eyes. "It's you I want to talk to, Rhi."

Rhi didn't feel up to any of this. Now all she needed was for Eve to suspect what was going on between her and Max, and she might as well pack her bags and catch the next boat out of Heartside harbour. What was Max thinking of, smiling at her like that with Eve standing right beside him?

"What?" she snapped.

Max pulled out his phone. "I did a video montage to go with your demo. I put it on the internet for you this morning."

Rhi stared at the images scrolling across the phone screen that Max was holding under her nose. She felt a confusing mix of emotions at seeing herself laughing over an ice cream on the beach, walking on the cliffs, dancing at the Heartbeat with her head thrown back and her arms held up high. . . Confusing because she remembered all the occasions when the pictures had been taken. She remembered the kisses that had followed most of them as well. Max had shot them when they were still going out together. She felt embarrassed, pleased, sad and happy all at the same time.

"Um, thanks," she mumbled, horribly aware of Eve beside her. "You didn't have to do that."

"Well guess what? I did," Max said easily. "I've uploaded the montage and your songs on a number of music sites. You've had hundreds of hits already."

Rhi gulped. Her songs were out there? With these pictures? And had Max said *hundreds* of hits? That was . . . huge.

"Are you serious?" she said weakly.

Max laughed. "Of course I'm serious. What will it take for you to believe in your own talent?"

Rhi stared at the photo montage again, still scrolling across the little screen. She looked so happy. She hadn't felt that good in ages. Even after the whole business with Andy Graves. What was the matter with her? Why couldn't she enjoy herself any more?

Her phone rang.

"Is that Rhi? Susi Wilks here, Andy Graves' PA. I'm calling to fix a time for your makeover. Will tomorrow after school suit?"

"Um," said Rhi, panicking at the sudden sense of freefall. "Yeah, well—"

The PA cut in briskly. "Four o'clock it is. There will be a team of professionals waiting for you. Don't be late."

Listening closely, Eve jabbed herself in the chest with her thumb.

"Um, great," Rhi stuttered. "Can . . . can I bring a friend?"

"Bring as many as you like. But don't be late."

The buzzing sound of the dialling tone told Rhi that

Susi Wilks had rung off. She stared stupidly at the screen for a few seconds.

"Andy Graves wasn't messing around when he said the music industry moves fast," Eve observed, her eyes gleaming with excitement. "Tomorrow?"

Rhi rubbed her temples. "I don't have anything to wear," she groaned. "And how will I get there?"

"I'm sure Polly will sort you out with one or her funny boho numbers," said Eve. "We'll borrow Dad's car and the driver again. I'll tell him to pick us up from the school steps."

"Leave it to Eve, Rhi," said Max. "She'll sort everything out. So it's really happening for you! Well done, superstar!"

He folded Rhi into a warm bear hug which seemed to go on for a lot longer than necessary. Rhi didn't know what to do with her hands. She wanted to hug Max back and breathe in his special smell. But she *couldn't* hug him back, not with Eve standing so close. She limited herself to a couple of weak pats on Max's shoulders.

Pulling back as casually as she could, Rhi sneaked a glance at Eve. Could she see the first inkling of suspicion on Eve's beautiful face? Was that little frown appearing between her neatly plucked eyebrows aimed at Rhi, or at Max, or at life in general?

Rhi realized that she didn't want to know.

SIXTEEN

Rhi gazed out of the car window, deep in thought. In twenty minutes, she would meet the people promising to transform her into a megastar. People with real-life contacts in the real-life world of music. The world Rhi so badly wanted to make her own.

Lila sighed with contentment and leaned her glossy brown head against the leather upholstery as Eve's dad's big car purred through Heartside. She patted Rhi's leg. "Are you excited?" she said eagerly. "Polly's got some amazing outfits for you, I know they'll go nuts when they see you wearing them."

Rhi had seen the dresses Polly had customized for her. They were every bit as gorgeous as the angel dress and the zombie dress Polly had made for the weddings.

Probably even better. She had tried them on at Polly's house last night, standing still as patiently as she could while Polly stuck pins under her arms and Lila turned up the music and danced around by the window.

"Hmm?" said Rhi now. "Oh. Yes. Of course I'm excited. Who wouldn't be?"

Right now she felt like she had a large rock sitting in her stomach. She wished they were going to the Heartbeat instead of Andy Graves' massive house in Cliffside.

"It's going to be like *The X Factor*," Eve pronounced, brushing her hair vigorously and then tucking the brush back into her tiny clutch. "They'll wave their magic make-up wands and turn you into someone else, Rhi. You won't recognize yourself when they've finished."

That's what I'm afraid of, Rhi thought.

"*X Factor* shmex-factor," said Polly. "Rhi's better than that."

The X Factor always made Rhi think of a sausage factory of identikit boys, girls and songs. Was that her fate? To be a flash in the pan? A one-hit wonder? She balked at the thought. But she couldn't speak. Her throat was too dry, and her brain too confused. She shook her head, feeling impatient with herself. She was in a position millions of girls would *kill* to be in right now.

Polly and Lila craned their necks in excitement as the big car swept up to the grand white floodlit gates of Andy Graves' beach house. Lights were on all over the house. Rhi could hear laughter, and pumping electronic music. She got out of the car on shaky legs.

A slim girl in neatly coiled dreadlocks and a red jumpsuit opened the big front door, clipboard in hand, in a blast of loud music. She flicked dark, beautifully made-up eyes over Eve, Lila, Polly and Rhi as they stood in a nervous huddle on the doorstep.

"Which one of you is our girl?" she asked.

Rhi felt the others pushing her forward. "I'm Rhi," she said. It came out in a squeak.

The girl smiled briefly. "Susi Wilks. Andy's not here yet, but the rest of the team can't wait to get started."

They all followed Susi Wilks through the big hallway. Rhi clutched her bag of outfits close to her stomach. It felt like a lifejacket in a stormy sea. There were people *everywhere*. Rails full of clothes. A large trunk full of what looked like hair products. Make-up cases. Wires trailing around the floor, and at least five different hairdryers waiting on a table.

"Gorgeous!" exclaimed a muscular man in a tight blue vest as Rhi and her friends entered the living room. Rhi wasn't sure, but it looked like he was wearing eyeshadow. "I don't know which of you Andy's lined up for the slaughter but I could eat you *all* for breakfast."

"It's this one, Gary," said Susi, flicking a finger in Rhi's direction. "The rest of you? Take a seat. There's drinks, nibbles, magazines."

"Well, we have plenty to work with, don't we?" said Gary, fingering Rhi's hair and sucking his teeth. Rhi felt like a dog in a show.

The room had been set out like a beauty salon. A rail of clothes stood to one side, while a large reclining white leather chair stood before a huge mirror studded with lights.

"How long is Andy going to be, Susi?" Gary called.

"Who knows," came an answering shout from the kitchen. "He was seeing EMI this afternoon."

"Typical," Gary sighed. "We'll do what we can until he gets here."

Rhi found her voice. "We've had a few thoughts about my look," she began hesitantly, looking at her friends for support. "My friend Polly, the blonde one" – Polly waved – "she's put together some great outfits that sum up my style. Do you want to see them?"

"Be my guest," Gary said.

Rhi held up her bag of outfits. "Where can I. . .?"

There was no way she was changing in front of this guy, or any of the other shadowy figures scurrying around the room.

Gary giggled and flapped his hands. "Don't mind me, darling. I've seen it all before."

"I'm sorry, I'm sure you have," Rhi ploughed on bravely, "but I haven't, so. . ."

"Go next door," said Susi Wilks, appearing as if by magic through a door Rhi could have sworn hadn't been there a moment earlier. "There's a long mirror you can use. Andy will be here as soon as he can."

Lila, Polly and Eve followed Rhi into the room Susi had indicated. Even Eve seemed cowed by everything that was going on.

"This is really serious, isn't it?" said Lila with a nervous laugh.

"Yup," said Polly.

Rhi pulled on her favourite piece, the playsuit with bluebird-shaped patches that Polly had sewn all over it. With a pair of aviators and some wedges, she felt pretty good. Fluffing up her hair, her confidence returning, Rhi twirled for the others.

"What do you think?"

"A bit Farmer Joe for me," said Eve, wrinkling her nose.

"It's a good thing I didn't make it for you then, isn't it, Eve?" Polly countered. She gave Rhi a wink.

Rhi felt a wave of love for her friends. "Ballgowns aren't really my thing, Eve." She put her hands on her hips. "I'm more of a hoedown gal."

"Darling," said Eve earnestly as Lila burst out laughing, "ballgowns are *everyone's* thing. You just have to find the right one, not to mention the right occasion."

Rhi hopped out of the playsuit and pulled out item number two: a soft grey shift dress. It looked completely awesome over the top of deep purple leggings. She left her feet bare.

"The Glamour Awards, this is not," sighed Eve, shaking her head.

"She doesn't want to be glamorous," Lila pointed out. "She wants to be Rhi."

This was a lot more fun than Rhi had been expecting. "I wanna be Rhi," she sang, giggling. She spread her hands either side of herself and waggled them jazz-style. "I wanna be me. Oh I wanna be Rhi. . ."

"Very kooky, chicken," said Gary, popping his head round the door. "Ready for the face?"

Wondering when Andy Graves would show up, Rhi happily settled herself down in the big white chair. Gary hummed to himself, selecting colours from an enormous trunk of lipsticks, blushers, mascaras and eyeliners. Several people in black polo necks stood around, whispering in groups.

"What's the name of the band, darling?" Gary asked, painting Rhi's cheeks with something that felt light and cool.

Rhi had no idea. A flash of unease rippled through her gut. What was she doing here, if she didn't even know the name of the band she was going to sing with? She wasn't even sure she liked their music.

"I don't think they've decided on a name yet."

"What kind of music do they play?"

Rhi didn't know that either. "It's . . . hard to describe." *That was true at least*, she thought with a nervous giggle.

Gary painted her eyelids with a shimmery mauve powder, then whipped a mascara wand up and down her eyelashes. Twirling her chair round, he raised his neatly plucked eyebrows (he *was* wearing eyeshadow, Rhi saw now) at Lila, Polly and Eve.

"What do we think, loves?"

Lila clapped. So did Polly. Eve folded her arms and ran her cool grey eyes from the top of Rhi's head to the tips of her bare toes.

"Sweet," she said eventually. "If folksy farmhands are your thing."

Gary whistled. "Get you, pussy cat with claws. Have you considered a career in the fashion business?"

Over the next couple of hours, they played around with several different looks. Rhi liked the more natural approach, with a peachy face powder that seemed to enhance the sprinkle of freckles across her nose. Eve read the fashion and music magazines scattered on the low tables while Polly and Lila buzzed around Rhi making noises of delight.

"Stunning!"

"Babes, you look incredible. Your eyes are like Bambi's!"

The front door banged open and the shadowy make-up artists and stylists and photographers all went into a busy huddle, with much clicking of heels on the wide uncarpeted floors, as Andy Graves strode in. Susi Wilks was beside him in a flash, taking off his coat. He took one look at Rhi – and to her horror, he burst out laughing.

"Oh dear girl, you are adorable! The boho look is out. Dead. Gone. I want high-voltage, not chicken feathers. Gary, Gary, Gary," he added, wagging a finger at the make-up artist, "have you lost your senses? This is not what we discussed."

Gary raised his muscular shoulders in apology. "We were playing around, boss. Waiting for you to arrive."

"Lucky I got here when I did," said Andy Graves. "You'd have put her on a combine harvester for the photos."

Rhi felt as a small and insignificant as a flea. From feeling on top of the world, she suddenly wished she could disappear into the padded white leather of the stylist's chair.

"Now," Andy Graves began as Susi Wilks pressed a glass of sparkling water into his hand, "I have been in a meeting this afternoon discussing a review of successful pop singers in the last two years with accompanying market research. Based on what I have learned, this is the approach we are going to take. Beka, I want you to bleach Rhi's hair ice-blonde and crop it really short. Then—"

Rhi exchanged shocked looks with her friends.

"You . . . you want to crop my *hair*? But I don't want—"

Andy Graves flowed on as if Rhi hadn't said a word. "Short hair is much easier with the wigs I will have designed for you. This –" he flicked his fingers at her outfit "– will never do. Chanice! Karmel! Loyd! Where's the body-con wardrobe I asked you to put together?" A rack of brightly coloured clothes in lurex, neoprene and PVC was wheeled into the room. Rhi stared at them. They all looked very tight. And revealing. One bright red dress appeared to be made of rubber, and seemed to consist of one strap across her breasts and another around her hips.

A punchy techno-pop beat suddenly filled the room, bumping and grinding through the large speakers set on either side of the white marble fireplace.

"I give you . . . Shox," Andy Graves said, adjusting the volume so the beat pumped even more loudly through the room. "Your new band. You are going to be a sensation when I've finished with you, Rhi Wills."

Rhi was at a loss for words. This was not the plan.

How much was she willing to sacrifice to follow her music dream?

SEVENTEEN

Andy Graves' fashion stylists swarmed around the white leather chair. They poked and prodded and talked about Rhi as if she wasn't there at all.

"She's a bit heavy, isn't she?" Chanice had ice-blue eyes and long white-blonde hair pulled back into a plait that fell almost to the floor. "Andy, you'll have to put her on a diet. These outfits are unforgiving on muffin tops."

Boom, boom, boom went Shox on the sound system. The singer – ex-singer, Rhi guessed, given Andy Graves' plans – screamed over the top. She couldn't make out many words, but thought that she caught *ooh* and *booty* and, possibly, *licks*.

"Let's try the black leather catsuit," said Loyd,

a handsome man with a half-shaved head. "It's so butch."

Karmel – a small, pretty Asian woman – plucked the catsuit from the rail and gave Rhi a brisk shove in the small of the back. "Time to take off the dishrag, darling. Be back here in five."

Aware of the watchful gazes of her friends, Rhi dumbly headed for the changing room, took off Polly's beautiful grey dress and pulled on the catsuit. It squeaked, and the tight leather cut into the backs of her legs.

"Now we're talking," said Loyd with satisfaction. He gave the front zip a brisk tug, revealing a lot more cleavage than Rhi felt comfortable with. He rummaged through a collection of shoeboxes and thrust a pair of shoes towards her. "These I think."

To murmurs of approval from the other stylists, Rhi slid on the highest pair of red platform spikes she'd ever seen in her life. Andy Graves looked up from his phone, and gave a brisk nod before returning to his call.

"You'll get used to the footwear, darling," said Loyd, noticing the panic in Rhi's eyes. "Gary? We need a look to match this. Biker, rock-chick, sex appeal, bad, dangerous. Kids love all that."

Rhi cringed as Gary selected a heavy foundation and a neon mascara and started laying pastes and powders thickly on her cheeks. She felt utterly powerless. Why didn't she speak up? Why couldn't she stop this? Surreptitiously she tugged her zip a little higher.

A skeletal girl with bright red buzz-cut hair – Andy Graves called her Beka – stepped up to the chair when Gary had finished. She pinned Rhi's hair painfully tight to her scalp, and then selected a blue wig with an asymmetrical fringe. Rhi could hear her muttering irritably under her breath as she tugged and heaved it over Rhi's thick curls.

"Up you get, darling." Gary gave Rhi a hand out of the chair. "Give your friends a twirl."

Rhi could barely stay upright, let alone twirl. Polly's eyes were as round as marbles. Lila had her hands over her mouth.

"You look incredible, Rhi," Eve said in awe.

Rhi didn't feel incredible. She felt like a trussed-up chicken in a blue wig. She looked beseechingly at Polly and Lila.

"Tell me honestly," she said. "What do you think?"

"It's very . . . now," Lila said carefully.

Polly frowned. "Can you even breathe?"

"Not much," Rhi confessed. She was nervous about breathing too hard. The catsuit zip felt as if it would plunge to her tummy button.

"You look sensational," said Andy Graves, sliding his phone into his pocket. It promptly started ringing again. "The press will adore you."

Rhi stared at herself in the mirror. A tall, leggy, sexy, fierce blue-haired girl stared back. It felt appropriate that she didn't recognize herself. Even without the dramatic makeover, Rhi had been keeping so many secrets lately, and asking herself so many confusing questions, that she hadn't known herself for days.

Who am I? What type of artist do I want to be? she thought, gazing into the biker-chick's neon mascara eyes.

The answer came to her at once.

Not this.

"Andy?" she said, before she lost her nerve. "I don't think this is quite . . . me."

A collective gasp ran through the room. Everyone stopped what they were doing and stared at her as if she'd just grown horns.

"Don't you want to be famous, Rhi?" Andy Graves enquired. "I know what I'm doing. Ask any of the acts I've worked with over the years. Trust me. This is what it takes. Take a seat in the chair, there's a good girl. Time to cut your hair. That wig is sitting on you like a toupee on a bank manager."

Beka approached, clippers in her hand. Rhi felt the blue wig being lifted off, and the blessed feeling of cool air on her head. The clippers started to buzz. The sound, and the horrified looks on her friends' faces, kicked Rhi into action.

"No," she said loudly. "I don't want to cut my hair."

Andy Graves sighed with irritation.

"Rhi, he said, "do you know how lucky you are to be here?"

Rhi swallowed. She couldn't let herself be bullied into this. "Yes," she said. "But I still don't want a haircut."

There was a sharp intake of breath from Chanice

and Loyd. Beka swung the clippers idly from one hand, watching and waiting for someone to make a decision.

Anger sparked in Andy Graves' eyes. Clearly, he wasn't used to being contradicted. "There are a million girls who would kill to have this opportunity," he pointed out. "I'm willing to be patient this once, but you have to decide, Rhi. I don't like wasting my time, and I don't work with amateurs. Are you willing to do what it takes to make it?"

Rhi felt terrible. "I'm sorry," she whispered. "I . . . I need to think about that."

Andy Graves sighed, and checked his expensive watch. "That's it for tonight, team," he said. "When Rhi has made her decision, we can come together again."

"Spoiled little girl," Rhi heard someone say — possibly Chanice. "Throwing her toys out of the pram."

Loyd grumbled, zipping away the body-con collection of clothes in a series of large black bags. Even Gary, the friendliest of Andy Graves' team, wouldn't meet Rhi's eye as he packed his make-up cases.

Rhi tottered to the changing room, kicked off the red spikes and wriggled out of the catsuit. A battle was raging in her head. She was a coward. This was her moment. She would regret it for the rest of her life if she didn't see it through.

As she came slowly out of the changing room in Polly's grey dress, Loyd whipped the catsuit out of her arms and stuffed it irritably into a zip-up bag with the rest.

"You're such an idiot," Eve hissed at Rhi as a silent Susi Wilks showed them to the door. "You've come this far, and it's like you want to throw it away. Don't you realize what this guy is offering you?"

Rhi turned to the others, desperate for some advice that she felt comfortable with.

"You have to do what feels right for you," Lila said, squeezing her arm encouragingly. "You did look . . . well, kind of amazing. But if you didn't like it. . ."

"You're more than a coat hanger," Polly reminded Rhi as Paulo the driver opened the passenger door and waited for them to get into the car. "This isn't just about the look. It's the whole thing. It's the music. So ask yourself this, Rhi. What do you want to do?"

That's the problem, Rhi thought hopelessly. *I don't know!*

EIGHTEEN

"Rhi! Can you come down here, please?"

Rhi's mother sounded stressed, as usual. Rhi pushed away her homework – she'd been having trouble concentrating anyway – and headed down the stairs.

Her parents were standing together in the study.

"What?" Rhi looked from her mum to her dad and back again, a flutter of unease in her stomach. "What's happened?"

Her father smiled. "Nothing to worry about, Rhi."

"Nothing?" echoed her mum. She tapped a key on her computer. "You call seeing your daughter plastered all over the internet *nothing*, Patrick? Rhi, can you explain this to us?"

Rhi looked at the computer screen. She saw herself laughing in the Heartside to the familiar sound of "Heartbreaker". As she watched, the picture dissolved into a thousand pieces, resolving itself into a moody one of Rhi on the beach with her hands in her coat pockets and the wind blowing wildly in her hair. The music played on. "Let me go, make me stay, Heartbreaker, show me a way. . ."

It was Max's photo montage. Rhi's music video.

"How did you get this?" Rhi said, half embarrassed and half pleased. Had her parents googled her? Were they maybe starting to get more interested in Rhi's music plans?

"An email was waiting for me when I got in from work," said her mother, dashing that particular hope. "It linked to this." She stared at the dissolving, spinning pictures of Rhi as if she'd never seen her daughter before. "I'm so *embarrassed*. It's had over five hundred views, Rhi. All those people know about it, and your own parents didn't."

"Why didn't you tell us, love?" said her father, more gently.

You'd know about it if you ever listened to anything

I said, Rhi thought. She shrugged. "I didn't think you'd be interested."

"Of course we're interested!" said her mother, sitting down abruptly at her desk. "Interested in stopping you from throwing your life away! That scout of yours sent over the contracts today. He wants you to sign away your entire life." She waved a sheaf of closely typed paper under Rhi's nose. "It's a pretty song, but really, Rhi? You're not thinking straight."

Rhi swallowed. Her throat felt thick with tears. "It's what I want to do," she said in frustration.

"You're fifteen years old," said her mother. "You don't know what you want to do. But I can tell you this. Six months down the line, when all the glitz and the glamour has worn off and your scout has got bored of you, do you know what will happen? He'll throw you on the scrap heap and move on to someone else. And there won't be a thing you can do about it. He will *own* you. All of you."

"I want to do this!" Rhi said furiously. *Do you?* whispered the voice in her head. The voice of all her doubts and fears. Ruth's voice. Rhi pushed it aside. "Why can't you understand that?"

"We're trying, love," said her dad. "But your mother's right. This contract is bad news."

"Of course I'm right," said her mother. "I'm *always* right. I most strongly advise you not to sign this, Rhi."

The more her mother went on about what a bad idea all this was, the more, perversely, Rhi wanted to do it. She snatched the contract from her mother's hands and held it closely to her chest. "I'll sign it if I want to," she said. "Andy Graves wants me, Mum. *Me.*"

"He wants a doll to dress up and push around," said her mother forcefully.

Rhi winced. Her mother was closer to the truth than she realized. She reminded herself of everything Andy Graves was offering. Somehow it felt dimmer and more unreal than ever – even now that she was holding the contract that would make it all happen.

"We do want the best for you, Rhi," said her dad.

The best for me? Rhi thought hopelessly. *Or the best for you?* She didn't know. She couldn't work it out.

The doorbell rang.

"I'll get it," said Rhi's dad.

He looked relieved to escape the sticky conversation.

As he headed to open the door, Rhi was left with her mother and the "Heartbreaker" montage on a flickering loop. Her mother's face looked tight, her skin yellowish with exhaustion.

"Are you OK?" Rhi felt compelled to ask.

Her mother straightened her shoulders. "I'm OK," she snapped. "It's *you* we're worrying about."

There was a cheerful bellow from the hallway.

"Anita! Come and see who's popped round to visit!"

Rhi followed her mother out of the office. Her legs almost gave way beneath her to see Max standing on the doorstep, his dark hair blown and wild and a flush of colour along his cheeks. *How can he still take my breath away?* she thought in frustration. *After everything that's happened?*

"Good to see you, Mr Wills," Max said warmly, shaking hands with Rhi's dad. "Hi, Mrs Wills. Do you know, you look as gorgeous as your daughter?"

Rhi's mother's pale cheeks pinkened with pleasure. She had always loved Max, Rhi knew. "What a lovely surprise!" she said, sounding almost girlish. "Isn't it a lovely surprise, Rhi?"

Rhi had no idea what to say. The sight of Max in the hallway had once been so familiar. Now it felt – alien. From some kind of parallel universe, over which she had no control.

"I was just passing," Max said, looking directly into Rhi's eyes. "Is this a bad time?"

"It's never a bad time to see you," said Rhi's mother at once. "Come in! Rhi, take Max's coat, for heaven's sake. Do I take it that you two are back together?"

Rhi wanted to sink through the floor. She caught Max winking at her.

"That would be telling, Mrs Wills," he said with one of his most dazzling smiles.

Rhi wanted to kick him. He was so . . . slick. What was he *doing* here?

"I won't ask any more," said Mrs Wills, tapping her nose in a way that made Rhi cringe. "You'll stay for dinner?"

No! thought Rhi in alarm. The last person she wanted to sit opposite for dinner was Max! But her mother seemed so happy, so different from the stressed, yellowish creature in the office just now, that she didn't have the heart to protest.

"That's really kind of you, Mrs Wills," said Max, sounding genuinely pleased. "I'd love to. If it's OK with Rhi?"

Rhi shrugged. Her mother frowned, giving her best *Be a little more encouraging!* face.

"Great!" said Max. "I always love the cooking in this house."

"Chicken curry tonight," said Rhi's dad. "Sound good?"

"Perfect," Max said warmly. "I really only came round to show Rhi another video I created for her. Did you get the link I sent you, Mrs Wills? Doesn't she sound fantastic?"

Rhi's mother was still beaming at the sight of Max. "Oh, did you put those pictures together? We were just listening to the songs. They're lovely."

News to me, Rhi thought, fighting the urge to roll her eyes towards the ceiling as she hung Max's coat on a peg. Her mother was as transparent as glass.

"Your daughter is super-talented," said Max. "But you already knew that."

Rhi saw her mother had the grace to flush a little. "Of course we did," she said.

"I did," Rhi's dad corrected, pulling cutlery from the kitchen drawers. "You didn't."

Rhi watched her mother's mouth pinch up. "I never said she wasn't talented, Patrick. I am just struggling to see how she can make a living at it."

"Plenty of people do," said Rhi's dad. "I'm sure there's a way round it, Anita."

"There *isn't*. We can't have two dreamers in the family," Rhi's mother snapped. She gave a brittle laugh. "Family life, eh, Max? It's enough to challenge us all!"

This is my fault, Rhi thought unhappily. *My music is making them argue.* Her parents' marriage had barely survived Ruth's accident. She had the unpleasant sense that her parents were only staying together for her sake these days. Now everything felt as if it was fracturing again.

"I know what you mean," Max smiled as Rhi's dad gave him a plate of curry. "My dad's driving Mum mad with all the golf he plays at weekends. Mum hid his golf clubs in the laundry room last week. She says he doesn't know where the laundry room is, let alone his clubs."

"Your poor mother!" said Rhi's mum. "Thank goodness Patrick doesn't play golf."

"I have many faults," Rhi's dad agreed, "but golf isn't one of them."

Rhi shot a grateful look at Max as her parents both laughed. You could say one thing for her ex-boyfriend: he knew how to ease any tension.

The rest of the meal passed smoothly, Max laughing and joking with her parents as if he'd never been away. Rhi propped her chin in her hand and watched him. He had a dimple in one cheek that always caught her eye when he laughed. Max laughed a lot. She allowed herself to relax. There were worse ways of spending a Wednesday evening.

"There are definitely ways of making a living at music if you're as talented as Rhi, Mrs Wills," said Max as they cleared the plates. Rhi's dad went to the cellar to fetch some ice cream from the freezer. "I'm sure she has a future in music, if that's what she wants."

Rhi didn't look up from stacking the dishwasher. The last thing she wanted now was to see her mother's face all pinched and disapproving again.

"Perhaps you're right, Max," she heard her mother

say. "If this scout sees something worthwhile in my daughter and not in all those hundreds and thousands of other girls trying to make it then I suppose she would be foolish not to explore it."

Rhi looked up in disbelief. But before she could double-check that her ears hadn't deceived her, the phone started ringing in the hallway. Rhi's mother answered it.

"Hello, Eve dear. How are you?"

Rhi's stomach plummeted. What would Eve think if she saw Max here tonight, laughing and joking over chicken curry?

"I'm sorry, but Rhi can't come to the phone right now," Rhi heard her mother say. "Max is over for dinner. Yes! Isn't that nice? I'm so glad they're back together."

Rhi exchanged a horrified glance with Max, who was as chalk-white as the plate he was holding. She had never told her parents she and Max had split up because of Eve. It would have broken her mother's heart. But now . . . she wished she'd told her mother everything. That way, this conversation would NOT be happening.

This was bad. This was really, *really* bad.

"That was nice of Eve to call," said Rhi's mother, returning to the kitchen, blithely unaware of how Rhi's stomach had just turned itself inside out. "I said you'd call her back when Max had left."

Rhi's dad emerged from the cellar, holding a tub of ice cream. "What did I miss?" he said cheerfully.

As he set the tub down on the table, Rhi felt her pocket buzz. She took out her phone with shaking fingers.

BACKSTABBING TRAITOR.

NINETEEN

After a stilted goodbye with Max and a promise that she'd watch his new video, Rhi went up to her room after supper to stare unseeingly at the wall. She felt sweaty and nervous as she thought about Eve and that horrible text. She even thought of calling Eve to explain, but what would she say? *I'm not back with Max, although we've kissed a couple of times?* She put it off until it was too late to call. Then she struggled to get to sleep, tossing and turning and dreading the morning. When she finally drifted off in the early hours of the morning, her dreams were full of horrible confrontations and anger.

She felt jumpy the whole way into school the next

morning, convinced that Eve would appear around every corner.

Backstabbing traitor.

I didn't know he was coming! Rhi wanted to cry. But she knew she wasn't exactly blameless. She'd kissed Max twice behind Eve's back. She'd let him help her with her music video. She had been keeping secrets, and Eve would never forgive her for it.

When Rhi got to school, it was clear that something was wrong.

A group of backroom staff were standing in a serious-looking huddle at the reception desk, deep in conversation. Paranoia surged through Rhi, prickling down her back and turning her blood to ice. Eve had done something. She knew it. It was just Eve's style to get her revenge in the most public, humiliating way possible.

"Get to your classroom," barked a receptionist, seeing Rhi hovering at the main doors.

"What's happened?" Rhi asked in terror.

"You'll find out soon enough. Your classroom, now."

Rhi panicked the whole way down the corridor

to 10Y. Kids were loitering, talking excitedly. The atmosphere was feverish, almost wild. What had happened? Rhi's imagination was in overdrive.

She passed Ms Andrews' classroom, where thirty kids stood silently beside the door. The head teacher was in the classroom – Rhi could hear his distinct, deep voice. She glimpsed something in large red letters on the whiteboard.

GO HOME

A tumult of emotions surged through Rhi like a riptide. Three thoughts stood out from the swirling chaos in her mind.

Poor Ms Andrews.

The rumour was out.

Polly.

The head teacher saw Rhi frozen in the doorway. "Go to class, Ms Wills," he rapped out.

Rhi fled. Her heart was pounding. Who would write that?

She knew the answer as soon as she had asked the question.

Eve. She was the only one who knew.

Eve had always been unpredictable. But this? Hurting a teacher, hurting Polly, just to get back at Rhi for stealing Max? They weren't even together again – not properly. Then Rhi remembered Eve coming out of Ms Andrews' classroom earlier in the week. It looked extra-suspicious in the light of what was going on today.

Rhi's phone buzzed. She yanked it from her pocket. A picture popped on to her screen showing Ms Andrews, her blonde hair instantly recognizable, kissing a woman. A woman that maybe not everyone would recognize at first, but would work out eventually. Polly looked too much like her mother for it to be a coincidence.

Judging from the shocked laughter starting to ripple down the corridor, the sender had copied in the entire school.

Getting to class on time suddenly seemed unimportant. Rhi had to find Polly. Had she heard already? Had she seen the picture? How could Eve do something so terrible? Rhi checked the number the photo had come from, but her phone didn't recognize it. Eve must have used a different SIM card.

Rhi walked, fast and furious, looking in classrooms, dodging groups of laughing kids and winking phone screens. She felt crushed with guilt for causing it all.

She checked round the door of the girls' toilet, the one nearest the reception desk that was normally used by the younger kids. "Are you in here, Polly?"

She walked through, checking under stalls, and stopped when she reached a pair of familiar shiny brogues, laced with red.

"Polly?"

The toilet door opened slowly. Polly was looking as pale as her blonde hair. "Have you heard?"

Rhi nodded. Polly covered her face. "I don't know what's worse," she said through her fingers. "That Mum's been keeping a secret like this, or that she's dating Ms Andrews."

Rhi pulled Polly into a hug. Polly hugged her back, bursting into tears.

"People can be so h . . . h . . . horrible," Polly wept. "Poor Mum! Poor Ms Andrews. They don't deserve this. I don't know if I'm angry with Mum, or angry with the idiots who wrote that awful thing on Ms Andrews' board and sent that stupid picture."

"Don't be angry with your mum," said Rhi, holding Polly tightly. "The heart wants what it wants. We can't change that. Save your anger for –" she had been going to say *Eve Somerstown* but that took too much explaining right now "– for the morons with the camera and the marker pen."

Polly sniffed and wiped her eyes with the heels of her hands. Rhi pulled some paper towels from the dispenser and handed them over.

"Oh God, I look hideous," Polly moaned, catching sight of herself in the mirror.

"You'll be fine," said Rhi as reassuringly as she could. "Stick with me. We'll face them down together."

Polly nodded, and blew her nose. She smiled wanly at Rhi. "Thanks, you're a really good friend. And you're right about the heart thing. Mum hasn't been happy in such a long time. If this is what she wants, I'll get used to it. I just wish I didn't have to get used to it with six hundred kids all laughing at the same time."

"Just pretend you're a celebrity," said Rhi, trying to lighten Polly's mood. "Think of all the extra publicity. Front page news. Interviews on breakfast TV. It could all happen for you now."

Polly gave a sobbing laugh. "Sounds like the kind of thing you'll be using in your stellar music career," she joked feebly, wiping her eyes one more time.

Rhi felt encouraged. Polly was handling this better than she'd thought she would. Then she thought of Eve, conniving horrible Eve, and felt angry all over again.

She slid her arm through Polly's. "Ready when you are."

Polly looked frightened, but nodded. "Don't leave me, OK?"

"I'm not going anywhere," Rhi promised.

The first group of kids they passed were year eights, being ushered towards the hall. Ms Andrews' tutor group, minus Ms Andrews. Rhi wondered where the teacher was. Two kids at the back were looking furtive as they giggled over a phone. Polly stiffened miserably, but Rhi pulled her onwards.

They found themselves on the corridor containing

Ms Andrews' classroom. The door was open. Both girls heard the familiar *tap-tap-tap* of Ms Andrews' shoes on the classroom floor, and the sound of books being taken off shelves. Polly slowed.

"I'm going to see if Ms Andrews is OK," she said, swallowing.

"Good for you," said Rhi. "I'm right behind you."

The teacher was slowly packing books into a cardboard box on her desk, her blonde hair swinging round her face. She glanced round, startled, as Polly and Rhi entered the room.

"I wanted to say how sorry I am about everything, Ms Andrews," Polly blurted, fiddling with her jumper. "And . . . and that I don't mind. About you and my mum."

Ms Andrews' eyes were red. It looked like she'd been crying. "Thank you, Polly," she said, clearly moved. "That means a great deal. This kind of thing is never easy. I'm sorry you had to find out this way." She gestured vaguely at the whiteboard, even though the message was no longer there.

Rhi frowned at the box of books. "Are you leaving, Ms Andrews?"

"The head teacher has given me a leave of absence until all this is sorted out," said Ms Andrews. "I hope I'll be back before long. But. . ."

Rhi felt a lurch of shock.

"They're punishing *you* for this?" she said, bewildered.

Polly's eyes filled with fresh tears. "But you haven't done anything wrong!" she said. "You can't go!"

Ms Andrews pushed her hair out of her eyes and resumed her packing. "It's best for everyone, Rhi," she said quietly.

Rhi couldn't believe the injustice. Ms Andrews was leaving, and no one was doing anything about the person who had done this to her! Dumbstruck, she could only stand and watch with Polly as Ms Andrews put the last items into her box and picked it up.

"Goodbye, girls," she said. Tears glimmered in her eyes. "Thank you for your support."

Something cold and hard settled in Rhi's heart as Ms Andrews left the classroom with her head bent over her possessions. A sense of resolve and purpose that she couldn't remember ever feeling before. For the first time in her life, Rhi wanted a proper fight.

And she knew exactly where to find one.

TWENTY

Rhi leaped out of her skin every time the door of the Heartbeat opened. She'd invited everyone she could think of to come after school. Everyone except. . .

Lila patted Rhi's arm. "Stop jumping like a startled horse all the time. I'm going to spill my coffee in a minute. For the third time, Eve doesn't know about this, OK? So just relax."

Rhi jumped again as the door swung open. More familiar faces flooded in, waved and took seats around the room. "Sorry," she said helplessly. "I just . . . you know what Eve's like. Popping up where you least expect her."

"What's she done this time anyway?" Ollie asked curiously.

Rhi wasn't prepared to accuse Eve out loud. Not yet. Not until she had definite proof. "I don't know for sure," she said carefully, "but if I'm right, it's bad. Hey, Polly!"

Polly had come through the door with her chin tucked into her coat. She looked exhausted. Keeping her eyes on the floor, she made her way towards Rhi and the others.

"We were going to walk with you," said Lila anxiously. "But we didn't know where you were."

Polly's big hazel eyes were red-rimmed and tired. "I took a different way here so I wouldn't see anyone. Rhi, do you mind if I sit there? Right now, looking at the wall is all I can cope with."

Rhi swapped seats, still half-watching the café door. No Eve. No Max either. It was time to relax, and focus on the reason they were all here.

"What's this about?" asked Ollie, echoing Rhi's thoughts. "My charm and good looks? Don't you get enough of those at school?"

"Are you going to sing again?" Lila asked eagerly.

Rhi studied her hands for a moment, gathering her courage. "I'm going to start a petition," she said,

185

looking up again. "To get Ms Andrews reinstated. It's a total scandal that she's been sacked."

"She hasn't been sacked," Lila said. "She's on leave until the fuss dies down."

"OK, so not sacked," Rhi amended, "but she's not allowed to work at the moment so it may as well be a punishment. Where is the justice in that? There's no law against teachers going on dates with parents. *Single* parents, I might add. The person who should go on indefinite leave is the one who wrote that horrible message on Ms Andrews' whiteboard, and sent that picture to everyone."

"Don't remind me," said Polly, who had put her head on the table between her hands.

No one was shouting her down about this. Feeling encouraged, Rhi pulled three clipboards from her bag. She had spent her lunch break composing the petition, with neat columns for people's names and contact details, and had a stash of biros which she handed round.

"Go round the tables in here and ask people to sign this," she said, handing Lila and Ollie a clipboard each. "The person with the most signatures at the end gets a free drink."

Ollie looked startled. He stared at the bar, where Ryan was offering a cheerful thumbs-up.

"I cleared it with Ryan earlier," Rhi explained. "In school."

She offered Polly a clipboard. Polly shook her head apologetically.

"I'm not up to it," she said. "Sorry."

Rhi had been expecting that, but had wanted to give Polly the option. She nodded. "Fine, I'll give it to Ryan. If this goes to plan, we'll have Ms Andrews back at school by the end of next week."

Lila and Ollie headed in opposite directions, clutching their clipboards.

"Will you be OK by yourself, Polly?" Rhi checked.

Polly nodded, and put her head back on the table again.

Most of the people in the Heartbeat were in total agreement with the petition. Feeling heartened as she moved around the room, watching the list of names growing on her clipboard, Rhi realized that she wasn't alone in feeling shocked by the situation. It was a good feeling.

"Rhi! Hey, over here!"

Brody Baxter was waving at her across the room, his blond hair pulled back in a headband and a ragged-looking surfer T-shirt hugging his muscular torso. His fruit-sticker guitar sat propped against the wall. Rhi's heart jumped. She'd been so caught up in her plans for the petition that she hadn't factored in the possibility of seeing him here tonight.

"What's the buzz?" Brody asked.

Rhi showed him the petition, feeling shy. "Would you sign it?"

He took the pen from Rhi's outstretched hand and scribbled his signature on the clipboard. "Saw your videos yesterday," he said, handing the pen back. "I didn't know you wrote songs too. 'Sundown, Sunshine' is my favourite, but your 'Heartbreaker' is awesome too. Have you written any more?"

Was it really only two weeks since she and Brody had sung together? Rhi thought in a daze. So much had happened since then. She didn't know where to start.

Seeing her hesitation, Brody patted the chair next to him. "Sit down," he said. "Talk to me."

Rhi laid the petition on Brody's table and sank down beside him. He smelled warm. "I have a few more songs," she said, blushing. "But those three are my best. We just did them as a demo for a scout. But he turned out to be a fake. So we tried someone else, who turned out to be real."

"Sweet," said Brody, nodding. "Has he signed you?"

Rhi bit her lip. Maybe Brody was the right person to confide in. He knew about this world. He could advise her.

"He wants to," she said, "but he just wants my voice. Not my songs. And he wants to completely change how I look."

Brody frowned. "The dude's a fool. So what does he want you for?"

"To front a band he's got. They're called Shox." Rhi squirmed as she said the name. It really was terrible. "They're the next big thing, apparently."

Brody rolled his eyes. "Nobody knows what the next big thing is ever going to be. It's one of those facts of life. *Shox*? Seriously?"

Rhi giggled, covering her mouth with her hands. It felt wicked, laughing at something that Andy Graves was preparing to pour lots of money into. "They're not really my kind of music," she agreed between snorts.

"So you're signing with him or what?"

"I don't know." Rhi rubbed her forehead. "It's the hardest decision I've ever had, Brody. What if I choose the wrong thing?"

She felt his hand close over hers. "There's no such thing as wrong decisions. There's just paths, taking us to different places. The only rule I would offer is this. Stay true to your art, Rhi. The rest means nothing."

Rhi felt a spark go through her body. Brody's hand felt so warm, and so right.

"We should sing together again," he said, looking at her with his crystal blue eyes. "I'm at the Heartbeat this weekend. I'll learn your songs. I think they could work really well as duets. I don't know about you, but I felt a really great connection when we sang last time."

Rhi couldn't tear her eyes away. "Me too," she managed. "I felt it too."

Brody gave a dazzling smile, dropped her hand and leaned back in his chair. "Decision made," he said. "At least, for me. What about you?"

Rhi was suddenly blinded by a brilliant idea that

might solve everything. Her heart rate quickened as she thought it through, trying to find the flaws. There were none. She had nothing to lose.

She pulled out her phone before she changed her mind.

"You calling your guy already?" Brody asked, watching her. "Telling him you're a Shox girl all the way?"

Rhi held the phone to her ear.

"This is Andy Graves, leave a message."

"Hi, Andy, this is Rhi Wills," she said, trying to stay calm. "I want to invite you to a gig I'm doing at the Heartbeat Café in town this Saturday with a really talented singer songwriter called Brody Baxter. It would be great if you could be there. I want to show you what we can do."

Brody looked shocked as Rhi pocketed her phone again.

"You . . . did you just flag me up to your scout guy?"

"Is that OK?" Rhi suddenly felt worried. Should she have checked with Brody first?

"Rhi, that's more than OK." Brody was looking at her in amazement. "That's brave. That's awesome."

"Hope so," said Rhi with an awkward smile. "Otherwise I just kissed my future goodbye."

"Seriously awesome," said Brody. He thumped the table. "We are going to scorch it on Saturday."

Rhi felt light as a feather. Suddenly she didn't care about Andy Graves, or Shox, or any of it. She was going to sing her songs, right here in the Heartbeat, with Brody. That's all that mattered.

"Hey, Rhi, can I talk to you?" said Lila, tapping her on the shoulder. She nodded politely at Brody, who raised his hand in return.

It took Rhi a moment to float back to earth. "Sure. Is it about the petition? How are you guys getting on? I got a little distracted, but I'll be on it again in a minute. Brody and I are planning to sing here together on Saturday. Do you and Ollie want to come?"

Lila's eyes flickered. "Great, sure. But can I show you something first?"

Rhi started feeling uneasy. "What?"

"It's your video," she said. "I got talking to some guys at one of the tables near the back who said it had changed this afternoon."

"Changed? Changed how?"

"Like this," said Lila unhappily.

She held her phone out for Rhi to see.

"Heartbreaker" was playing as normal, but instead of Max's pictures of Rhi looking sultry on the beach and the clifftops, there were a stack of photos that Rhi hadn't seen in ages. Her with her bushy hair in pigtails sticking out sideways. Pulling dumb faces in McDonald's. Pointing at a fat red spot on her forehead and making faces for the camera. The pictures were all at least two years old. Rhi groaned in humiliation.

This had Eve Somerstown's troublemaking signature *all* over it.

TWENTY-ONE

"I can't believe Eve would do something like that," Rhi said angrily, walking beside Polly along the dark pavements. "It's one thing getting back at me at school, but this – this is my *future* she's messing with!"

Polly squeezed her arm. "Between us, we had most of the Heartbeat laughing tonight," she said gloomily. "If Eve thinks you and Max have got back together without telling her, I'm surprised she hasn't done something worse than this."

"This isn't the first thing she's done," Rhi growled. "I'm convinced it's Eve who wrote that message on Ms Andrews' board, and sent the picture."

Polly gasped. "*What?*"

"I'm sorry, Polly," Rhi said hopelessly. "I saw your

mum and Ms Andrews together a few days ago. I didn't know whether to tell you because I didn't know how you'd feel, and Eve found me in the bathroom when I was feeling vulnerable about everything, and . . . I told her. I'm really sorry."

"You *knew*?"

"I wanted to tell you," Rhi said uncomfortably, "but it was difficult, you know?"

Polly was quiet for a while. "And you really think Eve told the world about Mum and Ms Andrews to get back at you?"

"Of course!" Rhi said. It was so *obvious*. "Who else would it be?"

"I don't know, do I? But I don't get why hurting Ms Andrews would hurt *you*. Are you really good friends with her or something?"

Rhi felt a brief moment of uncertainty. She liked Ms Andrews, but wouldn't exactly have described her as a *friend*. She brushed the uncertainty away. Eve was devious. Who knew what went on in her mind half the time?

"Eve did it because she knew I knew and hadn't told you," she said firmly. "So I would get the blame for starting the rumour. Don't you see? I'm going to confront her tomorrow in class. I don't know what I'm going to say, but I have to say something. She can't get away with it!"

"Don't," said Polly.

"Why not?" said Rhi, feeling startled.

"I appreciate your support, Rhi, with the petition and everything you're doing," Polly said awkwardly. "But maybe it's best to back off now. Mum and Ms Andrews are adults. They'll figure it all out for themselves. Causing a scene won't help."

In the midst of her anger, Rhi sensed that Polly didn't want a scene like the one Rhi was suggesting. *She's probably been through hell today*, Rhi realized. *Me storming all over Eve and causing more trouble is the last thing she needs.* Her rage popped like a balloon.

"Was it . . . really bad at school today?" she said tentatively.

Polly pulled a face. "Pretty bad, yes. I feel really ashamed about it. Not about Mum and Ms Andrews, but about how I'm handling all the comments, and the giggling. It's a horrible feeling, knowing that I'm embarrassed by something that's making my mum happier than she's been in ages."

She rubbed the corners of her eyes. Rhi suspected she was pushing back the tears.

They walked the rest of the way to Polly's house in silence. Ms Andrews' car was parked outside, Rhi noticed. As they turned up the drive, her mouth fell open in shock.

Walking towards them, her red head bowed and her chin tucked into the collar of her coat, was Eve. She stopped by the gate and looked warily at Rhi and Polly.

"What are you doing here?" Rhi demanded, recovering.

Eve shrugged. "Private business."

Rhi felt the rage boiling up inside her. *All of this was Eve's fault.*

"How *dare* you come here!" she said fiercely.

"Rhi. . ." Polly warned.

Eve raised her eyebrows. "I wasn't aware that you lived here, backstabber," she said coolly. "Or that you made the rules as to who walked on Polly's driveway."

Get a grip, Rhi ordered herself. *If you lose it, Eve*

has won. It was difficult. All she wanted to do was leap on Eve and claw her like a cat.

"Love should never have to be hidden," Rhi said. Her voice shook, but she kept her tone low and controlled. "I love Max, Eve. I always have. You *stole* him from me. But I let you back into my life. I wish every day that I hadn't done that."

Eve's eyes shimmered. "You're the one sneaking around behind people's backs now, Rhi. How does it feel, not having your high horse to ride around on any more?"

"I am *not* sneaking!" Rhi couldn't keep her temper any longer. Polly stood frozen by Rhi's side. "And if you'd given me a chance to explain about Max being round at my house for dinner, I would have told you that."

"I don't care what you—" Eve began, but Rhi cut her off.

"I told Max weeks ago that I could only see him as a friend for as long as you were going out with him. I *told* him! *He* kissed *me*. Twice. And both times I told him to leave me alone. He's the one who keeps coming back, Eve. Hanging round in corridors, coming over to my house. What does that tell you?"

Eve flinched. Rhi knew with triumph that she'd hit home. She surged on, riding high on her rage.

"And as for Polly's mum and Ms Andrews. . ." Words almost failed Rhi here, but she rushed on. "What gives you the right to pass judgement on them? What gives you the right to spread ugly rumours, and send horrible pictures, and write vile messages on whiteboards for the whole school to see? I can't believe you would be so hurtful. Even you, Eve, must be able to see how much harm you have caused here. Why do you have to make everyone miserable? Why?"

Eve's face was paler than Rhi had ever seen it. She looked almost as if she had been carved out of stone.

"That's what you think of me?"

She asked the question so quietly that Rhi could barely hear her.

"Yes! And don't bother to deny any of it!"

Rhi watched, almost in a dream, as the red-haired girl's cool, composed face crumpled like a tissue. Her pointed chin shook. Tears streaked mascara down her marble-white cheeks.

Eve was crying.

"Leave me alone," she screamed, bringing her hands up to her hair in fierce, bunched fists. "I hate you all. You have no idea what you're talking about!"

Shoving Rhi violently to one side, Eve ran full-tilt through Polly's gate and away into the night. The frantic clattering of footsteps faded into the traffic noises of the evening.

Rhi exchanged shocked glances with Polly.

What had just happened?

TWENTY-TWO

"Whoa," said Polly at last. "Talk about a reaction."

Rhi was feeling very strange. Guilty, almost. *Eve started it*, she reminded herself. But the guilt remained, burning slow and steady in her gut. Eve had looked almost wild with misery, running away into the darkness. Had she got it wrong?

When was the last time she had sat down for a proper chat with Eve? Rhi wondered uncomfortably. Weeks now. Truthfully, they hadn't talked since Eve had started seeing Max. Even when Eve took Rhi to see Andy Graves, they had only talked about Rhi and her plans. Not Eve at all. Rhi's conscience squirmed.

There was no doubt about it: Eve was a complicated person. Two years of friendship, and Rhi wasn't much closer to understanding her now than she had been at the beginning. Spiky, mean, generous, spiteful, funny, lonely, beautiful, confident, lost. The words swirled through Rhi's mind.

"Do you think she's OK?" she said at last.

"She didn't look very OK to me," said Polly.

They walked slowly into the house, with Rhi looking uncertainly over her shoulder. What had made Eve explode like that?

Polly's mum and Ms Andrews were talking in the hall in low, serious voices. Polly's mum swung round, her cheeks flushed with guilt at the sight of her wan-faced daughter.

"Polly, love," she said hesitantly. "Are you all right?"

"It was a weird day," said Polly. She looked at Ms Andrews. "But probably weirder for you, right?"

Polly's mum gave her a clumsy hug. "I'm really sorry, Polly. It must have been awful, finding out about me and Beth like that. It's so stupid of me, I should have told you earlier, but—"

"I know," said Polly, nodding. "It was difficult. I've been hearing that a lot recently."

Rhi squirmed again. She wished she'd been honest with Polly about what she'd seen that day in Polly's kitchen. She wished she'd been more honest with Eve too, about what Max was doing. She'd done a lot of wrong-headed things lately.

"Hello, Rhi love," said Polly's mum. "Let's go into the kitchen. There are biscuits."

"Not many," added Ms Andrews. "We've already eaten most of the packet."

Rhi followed Polly, her mum and Ms Andrews into the warm kitchen.

"What was Eve doing here?" Polly asked as Ms Andrews filled the kettle and handed round what was left of the biscuits.

"It was the strangest thing. The doorbell went about half an hour ago, and Eve was standing there. I invited her in. That was OK, wasn't it?" Polly's mother looked worried. "I have trouble keeping track of when you two are friends and when you're enemies."

"Eve confuses everyone that way," Polly said. "Not just you."

Rhi's mind was still whirling. Friend? Enemy? What was Eve to her, exactly?

"Well," Polly's mother continued, "I couldn't believe it when she told us she'd used her family's influence to get Beth back at school."

Rhi felt like she'd missed a step. She looked at Ms Andrews in confusion. "It's all sorted?"

"Eve saw me leaving with my box this morning," Ms Andrews explained. "She wanted to know if I was going because of the message and the picture. I didn't think any more of it, but came round here to see Ginny."

"And eat biscuits," said Polly's mother, patting Ms Andrews' hand.

"And eat a *lot* of biscuits," Ms Andrews agreed.

"Biscuits fix everything," said Polly's mother.

The women looked at each other warmly and laughed.

This was too much information for Rhi. "Sorry," she said, trying to keep everything clear in her head, "*Eve* helped you?"

"I know, I found it hard to believe too," said Ms Andrews. "But while she was here, I got a phone call from the head. He was very apologetic about how he'd handled the situation, and invited me to return in the morning. It confirmed everything Eve had told us."

But Eve's the one who wrote the message! Rhi wanted to shout. *Eve sent the pictures!* She had been so sure. . . But what had she been basing her theory on, exactly? Seeing Eve coming out of Ms Andrews' classroom that one time? Expecting Eve to take her revenge, and assuming Ms Andrews was that revenge?

Rhi suddenly understood Polly's reservations. All of this had hurt Polly, and her mum, and Ms Andrews. It hadn't touched Rhi at all.

Great, Rhi thought wearily. *Yet another massive mistake, Rhi Wills. You're doing well today.*

"Oh, and Eve was able to find out who sent the photos," Polly's mother continued. "I have no idea how she did it, but those kids have been suspended from school."

"All's well that ends well," said Ms Andrews. "Even when it starts badly."

The women laughed again.

So Eve has a heart after all, Rhi thought. *Or maybe it's just more manipulation.* That was more likely, she decided hopefully. If it was manipulation, then maybe she had been justified in attacking Eve the way she had.

Somehow the thought didn't make Rhi feel any better.

"All gone," said Ms Andrews, peering into the biscuit packet. "I brought crumpets too, which we have yet to touch. Ginny, do you have butter and jam?"

"Afternoon tea," said Polly's mother brightly as Ms Andrews browsed the fridge. "I haven't had a proper afternoon tea in years. But I think we all deserve it today, don't you?"

Polly hadn't said much since they'd come in, Rhi realized. She was obviously finding the situation with her mother and her teacher a little strange. It looked to Rhi as if Polly's mother was trying extra-hard to be relaxed as well. It gave the whole occasion an odd atmosphere. Rhi wondered how she would feel if her parents started seeing different people. Particularly people that Rhi knew from another part of her life.

By the time everyone was sitting down around a plate of hot crumpets, the conversation was flowing more easily. They chatted about school, and Heartside, fashion and politics and films.

"We saw a shocking film last week," said Polly's mum, refilling the kettle.

"It wasn't shocking, Ginny," Ms Andrews protested. "It was just boring."

Polly's mother rolled her eyes. "You're such a *teacher*, Beth. We left for pizza halfway through," she confided to Rhi and Polly.

"Ms Andrews corrects us when we use the wrong word too," said Polly with a giggle.

"Like less and fewer," Rhi added. "Less work, fewer desks."

"I've had that one a few times," Polly's mum agreed. "Only more often in the context of more pizza, fewer anchovies."

"What can I say?" said Ms Andrews. "I'm an educator."

"Is that like a Terminator, but with a calculator?"

Polly laughed so hard at her mother's comment that she almost spat her tea out.

"Wash your mouth out, Gin," said Ms Andrews severely.

Rhi felt full and relaxed. Apart from the scene with Eve, it had been a great afternoon. She glanced at Polly, who was whispering something to her mother that was making her mum giggle hopelessly. It was clear that Polly's mum and Ms Andrews had a lovely, supportive relationship full of laughter and affection.

"Oh," said Polly's mum, wiping the tears of laughter from her eyes. "I can't tell you what a lovely afternoon this has been, girls." She took Ms Andrews' hand across the table and squeezed it.

Ms Andrews squeezed back harder. "It's such a relief, not having to hide our feelings any more," she said, smiling into Polly's mum's eyes.

Rhi and Polly exchanged a knowing glance. They both knew all about hiding feelings for people they weren't supposed to like.

TWENTY-THREE

Rhi loitered by the classroom door as long as she dared. It was unlike Eve to be late.

"Sit down please, Miss Wills," said Mr Morrison, glancing over at her. "We have a lot to get through this morning because of the assembly."

"What assembly, sir?" asked Rhi in surprise.

"The assembly I've already mentioned twice this morning," said Mr Morrison patiently. "The anti-bullying assembly?"

A couple of kids in the class laughed. Rhi blushed, and found her seat.

"Register," said Mr Morrison. "Nadia Abdullah? Lesley Atkins? Hannah Brown?"

"Here, sir."

"Back at you, sir."

"Here, sir!"

Rhi watched the door. No one came in. Where was Eve?

"Max Holmes?"

"Here, sir."

Max grinned across the room at Rhi. His smiles came so easily, Rhi thought a little impatiently, given everything that was going on. Did nothing freak that boy out?

"Lila Murray. Polly Nelson. . ."

Rhi wondered if Max knew what was troubling Eve. Something told her that he didn't. And even if he did, the smile he'd just given her sent out a clear message. Whatever Eve's problems were, Max wasn't interested. Was that just true when it came to Eve? If Rhi had a problem, would Max still grin like that?

"Eve Somerstown?" Mr Morrison looked round the room. Looking back at yellow note stuck to the register, his face cleared. "Absent. Daniel Stevens?"

Eve wasn't coming in. Rhi didn't know whether to feel relieved or extra-worried, and Mr Morrison had to call her name twice before she heard him.

"Ollie Wright?" the teacher finished.

"Yo, Mr Morrison," said Ollie.

"Yo yourself, Mr Wright," said Mr Morrison drily. "Good. Bags away, everyone into assembly. Quickly!"

The head was pacing on the stage, a large screen set up beside him, as the classes filed into the hall. Rhi noticed Ms Andrews was sitting near the front. Her red jacket made her stand out in the black-uniformed crowd, almost as if she'd worn her brightest colour on purpose. Her hair gleamed and her eyes faced steadily forward. A few kids glanced in her direction and whispered, but the sound was more subdued than yesterday.

Rhi felt a hand on her arm.

"Meet you at the back," Max whispered.

He headed for a row of chairs right at the back of the room. After a brief hesitation, Rhi followed. What did he have to say to her now?

"I wanted to show you this."

Max glanced around for teachers before pulling out his tablet. "Tell me if anyone's looking this way," he added in a low voice. "The last thing I need is for someone to confiscate this. Look, I redid your videos for you."

Rhi saw the original photo montage was back in place. She'd forgotten about the embarrassing selection of photos Eve had planted on the internet. *That* had been Eve's revenge, she realized awkwardly. She'd pretty much forgotten about it in her determination to blame Eve for the situation with Ms Andrews. She was such an idiot.

"And I've added some information about your gig tomorrow at the Heartbeat," Max went on. "The comments are flooding in. Everyone's really excited, Rhi. You're doing these songs, right?"

Rhi nodded, struggling with the familiar panicky sensation of being in a situation beyond her control. People were coming tomorrow, to hear her and Brody. Andy Graves might show up. People knew her songs now, and they still wanted to hear her. That was good, right? So why did she feel so nervous? Maybe it was just a natural state for performers. She would have to get used to that one, if she wanted to write and perform for a living.

Max slid his tablet away and took Rhi's hand. He squeezed it affectionately. "I'm so proud of you," he said. "Of everything you're doing. After the show, shall I come round to yours?"

Rhi pulled her hand away. Did she really have to explain all this again?

"Max," she began, "we have to be friends. Remember? You and Eve? Where is she today, by the way?"

Max shrugged. "I haven't talked to her since that evening at your place. I think she's probably got the message."

"Got the message?" Rhi echoed. "Max, she's your *girlfriend*. She needs to hear from you personally if you want to stop going out with her."

Max rolled his eyes. "Stop worrying so much, will you? God! Eve can look after herself. So I'll meet you after the gig?" He brushed a strand of Rhi's hair out of her eyes. "You're going to be so great," he said warmly. "I can't wait to hear you. I'll kiss you to death right afterwards."

Rhi had wanted this for so long, she couldn't quite believe that she was hesitating about it. She and Max could be together again on Saturday night. Everything would be back to how it had been before.

But did she want that any more?

Max had been incredibly supportive about her

music career, but he had cheated on her with Eve – and cheated on Eve with her as well. There was no way round that. *Can I really forgive him for that?* she wondered. She had a sudden flash vision of Polly's mum and Ms Andrews smiling into each other's eyes. Being there for each other. She realized with some amazement that she was having second thoughts about Max.

I deserve better than this, she thought. *Don't I?*

An image of Brody Baxter's crystal blue eyes floated into her head. She thought of the way he had listened to her doubts about the scout. The way he had touched her hand.

Rhi was thoughtful after the assembly. Leaving Max as quickly as she could, she made her way down the corridor, trying to catch up with Lila and Polly.

"Hey, superstar," said Lila. "Everyone's talking about your gig. Max's videos have practically gone viral. You're going to have a serious audience tomorrow night."

"Don't say that," Rhi groaned. "You'll terrify me into a cupboard."

Polly tapped a flyer on a noticeboard they were

passing. "There's no way out of it now," she said. "There you are."

RHI WILLS and BRODY BAXTER
Heartbeat Café
Saturday 8pm

"I ran off a hundred flyers on Dad's photocopier last night. He went a bit mental that the colour ink's all run out, but I told him it was for a good cause," Lila said.

There were flyers everywhere, plastered along the corridor walls. Lila and Polly had been busy this morning. Kids Rhi didn't know kept coming up to her on the way back to the classroom, asking her about the gig.

"Are you doing 'Sundown, Sunshine', Rhi?"

"I love 'Way Down Low'."

"Are you going out with Brody Baxter?"

Rhi blushed at that one. She hoped her friends didn't notice. Nerves were starting to consume her again. She felt like a tightly strung guitar, bursting to play its first pure note.

"That's *good* nerves," said Lila when Rhi confided

the way she was feeling. "You're going to be fantastic, Rhi. These are your own songs, and you'll be singing them with Brody Baxter. You two are made for each other. Musically, I mean."

Polly raised her eyebrows. "Maybe in other ways too."

"Seriously," Lila went on, "you made the most incredible team the other week when you sang 'The One That Got Away'."

Brody will be with me, Rhi reminded herself. The thought calmed her. *Andy Graves could be there too. Hopefully he'll see what kind of an artist I really am.* That thought turned her legs back to water again.

Tomorrow night. *Everything* hung on tomorrow night.

TWENTY-FOUR

Rhi was shaking all over. Did she seriously want to feel like this every day for the rest of her life? Maybe she should start taking her mother's suggestions about a proper job more seriously. A nice quiet desk in a nice quiet office had never looked so appealing.

She forced herself to look through a crack in the backstage curtains, and instantly wished she hadn't. She had no idea the Heartbeat Café could hold so many people! Squeezed round tables, on the balcony, covering every available inch of carpet. And *all* of them looking straight at the stage, waiting for Rhi and Brody to perform.

How do performers do this every day? Rhi wondered in terror.

She peeped again with a horrible fascination. Her dad was hovering near the back. Polly was at the front, sitting with her mum and Ms Andrews. Lila and Ollie were at their usual table, with several others including Max. Still no Eve. Rhi couldn't decide if this made her feel better or worse.

Her throat got even drier. Andy Graves was at a table right in the middle of the room, together with his assistant Susi Wilks. She tugged the curtains closed again. Backstage was too small. She wanted to fling open the fire door and run away, down to the sea, hide in a cave . . . anything but this—

"Hey, Rhi. You're trembling like a rabbit looking at a stewpot."

Brody smiled at her, adjusting the neck of his T-shirt with one hand, the other holding loosely on to his fruit-sticker guitar.

"I can't do this, Brody," Rhi stammered. "I know we've practised and everything, but there are too many people—"

He was by her side at once, stroking her back with his rough palm. "It's just adrenaline. It's there to sharpen you up, brighten your voice and focus your fingers. Let it flow through you, work its magic. I get worried when I'm *not* nervous before a gig. It usually means I'll mess something up."

Rhi gazed at him with big frightened eyes. "You're not just saying that to calm me down?"

"I'm not."

His hand felt nice, rubbing her back in regular circular motions. Rhi felt her breath steadying.

"I'll open the window," Brody suggested. "Fresh air will help."

Rhi hung her head out of the open window for a minute, closing her eyes and letting the wind blow through her sweat-dampened curls and cool her burning head.

Breathe, she told herself. *You wanted this. It's up to you to make it happen.*

Rhi heard Ryan Jameson's voice out on the stage.

"A warm Heartbeat welcome to what promises to be a fantastic night. We're showcasing two tremendous local talents tonight, and it's terrific to see so much support."

Rhi wanted to throw up at the sound of cheering. She squeezed hard on Brody's hand, which had snaked into her own.

"When we're out there, sing to me," he said softly, handing Rhi her guitar. "Forget everyone else. It's just us, Rhi. Us and the music."

Rhi gazed gratefully into Brody's eyes. He was just what she needed right now.

"So it's time to give a big cheer for . . . Brody Baxter and Rhi Wills!"

Rhi let Brody lead her on to the stage, into the deafening roar of appreciation. She kept her eyes firmly on him as he leaned into the mic.

"Hey. Good to see you all. We're going to kick off with a song by Rhi that you all know. 'Sundown, Sunshine'."

The roar that followed this announcement surprised Rhi. They really wanted to hear her song. Feeling reassured, she put her guitar round her neck. It felt like hers tonight, not Ruth's.

Brody kicked in with the opening chords. Rhi joined him, facing him, eyes for no one but him.

"Be my sundown, Sunshine," she sang.

"My sundown, run-up-to-sun-up Sunshine," Brody sang back.

"My moonrise, my night skies," they sang together,

one above the other in perfect harmony, guitars a heavy, strumming blur between them. "My twilight, my all night, my turn-off-the-light, my Sunshine, be mine, be mine. . ."

The crowd sang along. "My Sunshine, be mine!"

The cheers that followed the conclusion to the song almost made Rhi break down and cry.

"Good work, partner," Brody whispered in her ear, his breath warm against her skin.

They sang Brody's 'Fast Lane Freak' next. The crowd went wild. Rhi was enjoying herself so much she forgot the terror she had been feeling earlier.

"Trash and cash is all the same," she sang, playing with all she had.

"Everyone ride that gravy train. . ." Brody returned.

"Breathe the fumes and breathe the fame, I'm a fast lane freak, I ain't ashamed, I ain't ashamed," roared the crowd, swaying and thumping the tables.

This is me, Rhi thought exultantly. *I know who I am. And I like it.*

She and Brody repeated their cover of 'The One That Got Away' next. They had refined it, and Rhi had added a guitar line of her own. The crowd stilled, but still sang and murmured the lyrics under their breath. The connection was still right there, even better and brighter than before.

What is this thing that we feel when we sing? she wondered. *Is it just part of the performance, or part of something bigger?* It was so intimate, almost like kissing: the give and take, the teasing and the feeling that swelled in her heart every time their voices came together.

Throughout the song, she was aware of Max's dark eyes watching, warm and full of emotion, and focused entirely on her. Did she want to get back with him? Or was Brody. . .

She pushed any thoughts of romance with Brody out of her mind, concentrating on bringing the lovely song to its gorgeous conclusion. She didn't even know if he was interested in her that way.

"Back in ten, folks," said Brody.

He put his hand on Rhi's back and guided her off the stage. People were all around them, touching them, calling out to them.

"Beautiful."

"You just made me cry!"

"Are you doing 'Heartbreaker' later?"

Rhi almost crashed right into Andy Graves.

"Rhi Wills," said the talent scout warmly, "that was really beautiful. You have a terrific talent."

Rhi's face hurt from smiling. Andy Graves liked her. He understood her music at last! "This is my singing partner, Brody Baxter," she said breathlessly.

Andy Graves shook Brody's hand briefly, before turning back to Rhi again. "I've set up another meeting on Monday for you to meet Shox. We'll tackle the hair and the look at the same time. I have such great plans for you. We can—"

Rhi held up her hand. "Wait," she said. "You still want me to front Shox?"

Andy Graves looked surprised. "Of course I do. You and your friend write nice songs, but it's not the kind of music I want to produce. It's not commercial enough."

Rhi stared at his handsome face, his expensive clothes, his assistant hovering in the background constantly checking her watch. *He doesn't get it,* she realized. *He doesn't get it at all.*

She felt strangely liberated.

"Mr Graves," she said, smiling at him, "thank you for such an amazing opportunity."

He nodded, as if he'd expected nothing else. "Great. The meeting's set for four o'clock at my—"

Rhi interrupted. "But I'm not going to sign away my identity to you or anyone."

The smile faltered at the edges. "You're . . . not going to work with me?"

Clearly, no one ever said no to Andy Graves. His face was almost comical as he processed Rhi's decision. Rhi, on the other hand, didn't feel a flicker.

"I'm just starting to figure out who I am," she explained. "And I like what I see. Thank you again, but my answer is no."

She felt a hand pull her round and away from the perplexed-looking producer.

"Did I hear that right?" said Brody. "You turned the guy down?"

Rhi nodded. It was the strangest sensation, knowing and believing one hundred per cent in a decision like the one she had just made.

Brody made an appreciative noise in the back of his throat and pulled her into a tight hug. "You are awesome, Rhi Wills," he said into her hair. "You did the right thing. Your time will come. With a voice and a talent like yours, I know you'll make it your own way and no one else's."

The crowd was starting to get restless. "Brody and Rhi! Brody and Rhi! Brody and Rhi!"

Rhi didn't need Brody to pull her on to the stage this time, although she gladly let him.

"Thanks, everyone," she said down the mic. "I'm having the best evening of my life, seriously. We'll do a couple more songs for you, then I need a drink."

Everyone laughed. Rhi could hear her dad laughing loudest of all.

"The next song is called 'Heartbreaker'," she said. "Sing along if you know the words."

A happy sigh rippled through the room as Rhi bent her head over her guitar strings. It felt strange, singing something that had once been so private, and was now out there in other people's heads. She wondered briefly about Max again. She'd written the song about him. Was it a bad idea to get back with a guy who had broken your heart once already?

"Heartbreaker," she sang, "lead me astray. . ."

"Heartbreaker, show me a way," Brody chimed in, giving the gentle song that extra magic he always seemed to find.

Rhi watched Brody as he sang with her. The music had united them in a way she'd never experienced. Maybe their connection *was* more than a love song.

"Let me go, make me stay," sang the crowd, "Heartbreaker, show me a way."

Rhi smiled, losing herself in the music. She had made the right decision. She didn't want to be famous. She wanted to be honest.

The roof almost came off the Heartbeat at the end of the set. Rhi drank it in, smiling at her friends and blowing kisses to her dad. Andy Graves had left. She didn't care.

Brody blew gently on the back of her neck. "Way to go, partner," he said.

Rhi laughed and leaned in to him, hugging him tightly. In the midst of the cheering and applause, she felt something shift in the way Brody was holding her – like he didn't want to let go.

Rhi felt light-headed. She drew back and stared at

him. He stared back, serious now, twisting his fingers through hers. Her stomach flipped.

Brody was going to kiss her.

He leaned in. She felt a flutter in her heart as their lips just barely touched. It was so subtle that no one in the audience would have seen it, but to Rhi it was the most romantic moment of her life.

"Rhi!"

Max jumped on to the stage as Rih and Brody broke apart. He hugged her tightly, picking her up and twirling her around.

"You were incredible tonight," he said, sounding almost breathless. "The most beautiful girl in the room. I'm so proud of you! Hold on, I got you something. . ."

He leapt off the stage, rummaged around under the table and jumped back again before Rhi had time to move or react.

"Ta-da!" he cried, waving a gorgeous bouquet of deep red roses under her nose. The scent was overpowering. "I think they wilted a bit in 'Heartbreaker'. I did too." He wrinkled his nose charmingly. "I'm so sorry I hurt you, Rhi. I promise I'll never do it again. I love you so, so much."

Rhi burst into tears as Max put his arms round her again, squeezing her so tightly she could hardly breathe. Through tear-blurred eyes she saw Brody over Max's shoulder, packing up his guitar with his blond head turned away from them.

Something special happened here tonight, Rhi thought, so full of emotion she could hardly think.

But had it happened with Max – or Brody?

LOOK OUT FOR MORE

HEARTSIDE BAY

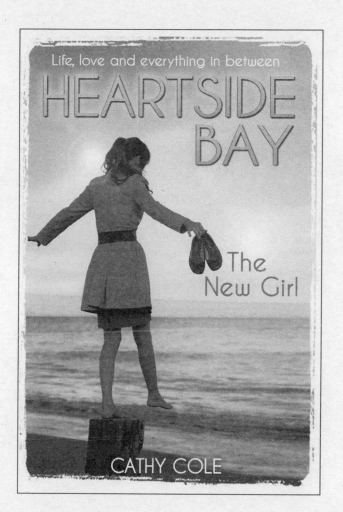

Life, love and everything in between

HEARTSIDE BAY

The New Girl

CATHY COLE

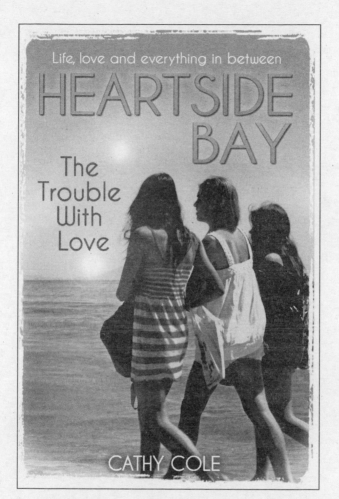

Life, love and everything in between

HEARTSIDE
BAY

The Trouble With Love

CATHY COLE